D1443182

CLOUDS over CALIFORNIA

WITHDRAWN

CLOUDS over CALIFORNIA

KARYN PARSONS

LITTLE, BROWN AND COMPANY
New York Boston

This book is a work of fiction. Names, characters, places, and incidents are the product of the author's imagination or are used fictitiously. Any resemblance to actual events, locales, or persons, living or dead, is coincidental.

Copyright © 2023 by Karyn Parsons

Cover art copyright © 2023 by Geneva Bowers. Cover design by Prashansa Thapa Cover copyright © 2023 by Hachette Book Group, Inc. Interior design by Michelle Gengaro

Hachette Book Group supports the right to free expression and the value of copyright. The purpose of copyright is to encourage writers and artists to produce the creative works that enrich our culture.

The scanning, uploading, and distribution of this book without permission is a theft of the author's intellectual property. If you would like permission to use material from the book (other than for review purposes), please contact permissions@hbgusa.com. Thank you for your support of the author's rights.

Little, Brown and Company
Hachette Book Group
1290 Avenue of the Americas, New York, NY 10104
Visit us at LBYR.com

First Edition: July 2023

Little, Brown and Company is a division of Hachette Book Group, Inc. The Little, Brown name and logo are trademarks of Hachette Book Group, Inc.

The publisher is not responsible for websites (or their content) that are not owned by the publisher.

Little, Brown and Company books may be purchased in bulk for business, educational, or promotional use. For information, please contact your local bookseller or the Hachette Book Group Special Markets Department at special.markets@hbgusa.com.

Library of Congress Cataloging-in-Publication Data
Names: Parsons, Karyn, 1968– author.
Title: Clouds over California / Karyn Parsons.
Description: First edition. | New York : Little, Brown and Company, 2023. | Audience: Ages 9–12. | Summary: "Stevie struggles to fit in at her new California middle school and is experiencing changes at home, while the Black Panthers and women's rights movements influence her life from the background."—Provided by publisher.
Identifiers: LCCN 2022031490 | ISBN 9780316484077 (hardcover) | ISBN 9780316497770 (ebook)
Subjects: CYAC: Moving, household—Fiction. | Middle schools—Fiction. | Schools—Fiction.
Classification: LCC PZ7.1.P3715 Cl 2023 | DDC [Fic]—dc23
LC record available at https://lccn.loc.gov/2022031490

ISBNs: 978-0-316-48407-7 (hardcover), 978-0-316-49777-0 (ebook)

Printed in the United States of America

LSC-C

Printing 1, 2023

For Yvette

Chapter One

I don't want to hear any more about it!" Dad says, the color in his cheeks rising with his voice. He waves a hand over his head, attempting to close the door on further discussion.

Mom quickly shushes him. "Keep your voice down. You'll wake Stevie."

But it's too late for that. I've been up for at least an hour while the two of them have been barking at each other. I don't know what happened. When I went to bed they were watching TV and laughing together. They were having a great time.

But now...

I tried to go back to sleep, tried to drown out the fighting by burying my head under pillows and stuffed animals, but they were just too loud. Then I thought that maybe if I came down to the kitchen, I could get them to stop. But once I got there, I couldn't figure out what to say or what to do. So, instead of doing anything, I'm just standing here. Hiding around the corner, hoping they'll stop.

"I just don't understand it," he says, turning his back to her and heading for the sink. "You've got everything you need. Everything all taken care of, and still, you want to go to school? For what?"

Oh, so this is what it's about. I've heard Mom talk to my aunt Mona about wanting to go back to school. To college.

"You got you a good man who provides for you all. Why on earth would you wanna do something like that?"

But Mom says she always feels like she missed out. I've even heard her say that if she got her "degree" she might be able to work. I wonder what kind of degree she's even talking about. What kind of work. She's never said anything about wanting to be a doctor or a lawyer or anything like that. And I wonder if she's told Dad that she wants to go to work. 'Cause seriously, if he gets this mad about her going to school, I can't imagine what he'd say to her getting a *job*.

Mom lets out a loud sigh, making her nostrils flare. "I've told you. It's only a couple classes. It wouldn't interfere—"

But Dad interrupts. "The only women that go to college

are there looking for husbands. And the men there know it. Is that it? Are you trying to find a boyfriend?"

A *boyfriend*? At school? What the heck is he talking about?

"Oh, Coop, you can't be that ridiculous!" Mom says, joining him at the sink, but he turns his back to her and fills a glass with water from the tap.

"Heck, I go to work, make sure we're taken care of, and when I come home—well...I want a home! What's wrong with that? *I* go to work—*you* take care of the house."

Mom says Dad is "old-fashioned," but sometimes he just seems plain unfair to me. I don't think I've ever heard *her* tell *him* he can't do something. Besides, what's wrong with Mom's wanting to take a few classes? What's the big deal?

"I move us into this nice place and—"

"Hold on!" interrupts Mom now. "I never asked to move," she says. "None of us *wanted* to move, Coop!"

I know *I* didn't want to move. I loved my old house. My old room. My best friend was just across the street. And my parents weren't fighting. *Why are they fighting?*

Dad turns to Mom and is about to say something to her when he spots me at the doorway. I guess I leaned a little too far into the kitchen. He doesn't say anything, but Mom sees his eyes land on me and quickly whips around.

"Stevie!" She makes a beeline for me but snaps at him from over her shoulder, "I told you you'd wake her!"

"You must think I'm stupid," he mumbles. Then he turns to her again. "I know what this is really about, Kitty. The only reason you want—"

This time, Mom waves a dismissive hand his way. "Oh, what is wrong with you?" She takes hold of my shoulders and leads me out of the room. "C'mon, pumpkin. You need to get back to bed."

As we exit, I turn and watch Dad simmer as he stares into his glass. "I won't have it!" he mutters. His face is red, and I swear I can hear his heavy breathing from all the way over here.

Once we're in the living room, Mom stops to drag a manicured finger under the corner of her eye, but I still see the tears there. It looks like she's cried all her makeup away.

"I'm sorry you had to hear that, Stevie, but don't worry. Everything's okay." But it's not. I can see it's not. "Want me to read a little something to you?" she asks, checking my face for any sadness that may have rubbed off.

I force a smile. The last thing I want is for her to worry about *me*.

"Sure," I say. Mom hardly ever reads to me anymore.

My room is peaceful, and I think I can feel Mom soften as we enter and cross to my bed. My night-light casts a cool glow on the floor and the moon beams in a strip of gold through a crack in the drapes. I push my stuffed toys to the floor and make room for Mom to scoot in next to me.

Over the head of my bed is a small shelf lined with all sorts of books, a dictionary, and the illustrated encyclopedia of the animal kingdom. Mom wants to read from the new book of funny poems she picked up from the library.

She launches into a silly story about a king and a peanut butter sandwich. She tells the story with a stuffy British accent, and I laugh through the whole thing. By the end, we're both cracking up.

"That was pretty good!" she says when she's finished.

"I liked it," I say. "It was funny."

"Another?"

"Please!" I pull my covers up to my chin and snuggle in close to her. Sleepiness creeps in and I surrender to it, so comfortable in my bed, my mom's voice gently coaxing me to sleep.

It must be hours later when a nearby siren cuts through my dreams and startles me awake again. I remember the fight. Mom crying. Dad so angry.

The room is dark and the entire apartment is silent.

Mom has crawled under the covers next to me and is softly snoring. On my bedside table lay her wig and long false eyelashes. I rarely get to see the tight little curls of her natural hair or her face free of lipstick and butterfly lashes. Like this, she looks young. She looks so pretty. And, like this, I think I can see my face in hers.

Chapter Two

Mom and I overslept! It's all because of that late-night fighting. And now I'm going to be late. Wouldn't you know it'd happen on the first day at my new school!

We race through our morning routine. Hummingbirds on fast-forward. No time for the first-day-of-school feast she'd promised. Corned beef hash and eggs, buttered toast and strawberry jam. Instead, it's Cap'n Crunch, two quick braids for my hair, brushed teeth, and out the door we go.

My new school is easily within walking distance, but there's no time for that. We hop in the car and Mom zips through side streets and rolls past stop signs. We hear the bell ring just as she screeches up to the gate.

"Okay, Stevie. The front office is right there." She points. "Tell them your name and that you're a new sixth grader.

They'll tell you where to go. I love you." She plants a kiss on my forehead.

"Wish me luck," I say, dread churning the juices of my stomach.

"You don't need luck! It's going to be a great day," she says and turns me to the wolves.

I scurry through the gates, but as I'm passing the hand-ball courts, I take a look over my shoulder. Mom is waiting and watching, just like I knew she would be. She waves and mouths, "Hurry up!"

I grin and give her one last wave. But as I approach the building, windows from the classrooms are filled with curious faces, all inspecting the late girl. The new girl. My grin quickly fades.

I always used to feel bad for new kids. They reminded me of baby chicks, freshly kicked from the nest, staggering to make their way around on wobbly legs. I don't think there's anything worse.

And now, that baby bird is me.

Once I'm inside, they make me wait in the office for what seems like an eternity while they locate my paper-work. Across from me sits a miserable-looking girl with a green snot ball hanging just below her left nostril. She's all mouth breathing and red-eyed. The snot ball moves up and down with her every breath.

Someone send that girl home!

Finally I'm summoned. "Come with me, Stephanie." A woman with short-cropped hair, a turtleneck, and an overbite walks me down a long, dark hall.

"Excuse me," I say. "No one calls me that. It's 'Stevie.'"

She glances back at me without missing a step.

"Like the boy's name?"

"Well, no. It's 'Stevie,' short for Stephanie."

"'Steph' is short for Stephanie. Or 'Annie.'" She gives me a quick once-over like maybe there's a name tag or a neon sign that bears the proper spelling of my name. As she jots something on the paper she's carrying, she laughs to herself and says, "Suit yourself. If you don't mind having a boy's name."

When we get to the classroom—an outdoor bungalow— Overbite Lady opens the door for me. I step inside and she gives the teacher a big fake smile.

"Stephanie Stevie Morrison," she says, handing the teacher my papers. The teacher nods to her and she promptly leaves, closing the door behind her without a word to me. No "Good luck" or "Catch you later" or even one of those phony smiles. She just dumps me off like I'm a sack of hot garbage.

I should've tripped her on her way out.

My teacher seems nice enough, though.

Mrs. Quakely is all teeth. She's got a huge smile. And she's super tall with feet that I'm pretty sure are bigger than my dad's.

"What a pleasure to meet you, Stevie," she says, stooping low, eyeballs wide and white as golf balls. She stands upright, takes hold of my shoulders, and turns me to face the firing squad. The kids in the class have been staring throughout our exchange, slack-jawed and glassy-eyed. As soon as Mrs. Quakely announces, "Class, we have a new victim!" I hear the boys snicker and the sandpaper-scraping sound of girls whispering. "This is Stevie. Show her love." And with that, she directs me to a desk *front and center* of the class. My cheeks flush hot and I turn to Mrs. Quakely, and then gesture to the empty desk in the rear corner of the room. I bat my eyelashes like Bugs Bunny, but she ignores my silent request for a seat out of the spotlight.

"*This* seat will be perfect!" she says, beaming.

Morning lessons start with history, and we each have to reach into a hat and pick a slip of paper with the name of the president of the United States that we'll be doing a report on. I was pretty sure after studying US presidents at my old school that I knew *all* of them. I know that George Washington was the first and Lincoln was the sixteenth. I know the difference between Teddy and Franklin D. Roosevelt, and that Benjamin Franklin was *not* a president, no matter how much the boys in class wanted to insist that he was . . . a whole bunch of stuff. But when I lift my slip of paper from the hat, I see a name that's as familiar to me as hieroglyphics.

John Tyler

Huh? Who the heck is that?

Around the room, kids start calling out who they picked.

"John Adams! Yes! Second president!"

"I got you beat! George Washington!"

"Andrew Jackson!" calls out one boy. "Twenty-dollar bill, baby!"

As they all compare and share their knowledge of each other's picks, I pray that my boring pick of a president isn't any indication of how this school year is going to go.

At recess, there's the usual interest in the "new kid." I know all about this sort of interest, but I'm reminded again that in the past, I've always been the one checking out the newbie.

The kids pass me with examining eyes, like they're taking in a new species or something. *Is it a lobster? A crawfish? Is a scorpion a crustacean? Whatever it is, is it nice? Is it safe?* I pretend their prying eyes don't bother me and instead wander over to the tetherball game.

11

At my old school, I was tetherball champ. Nobody could beat me. But I guess it'd be pretty weird for me to announce that now, so I plop down and watch. It isn't long before I figure out that the girl they call "Ally" is the champ around here. Her tangle of brown-and-gold waves whips across her face with every pounding of the ball, but she doesn't seem to mind. The other girls are more careful, studying the whiplash swirl of the ball, determined to find the best and most accurate way to attack it. But Ally is just ferocious. *SMACK! SLAM!* She doesn't wait or think. She *STRIKES*. And before the girl with the tidy yellow bowl haircut can land a fist on the ball, it's already wrapped itself completely round the pole and Ally has won again.

"Next!" she calls and shoots a look my way, but I quickly turn my head and pretend to be watching a group of boys wrestling each other nearby.

"My turn!" Another girl leaps from the blacktop to challenge Ally.

"Hurry up, then, Rachel!" says Ally.

Rachel is skinny as a zipper and wispy as the straight brown hair that hurries down her back to her butt. As she floats over to Ally, I'm pretty sure the champ is gonna finish her before she even lays a hand on the ball.

"Ready?"

Rachel nods and Ally *SLAPS* the ball hard.

It's *ONE* whip around the pole. Rachel's wide eyes and bony arms struggle to coordinate. But she misses her chance and Ally *POUNDS* it again.

TWO whips around. Rachel's arm is up high, but not fast enough to touch the ball.

THREE whips around. The ball is now traveling so fast that Ally just pushes it. Rachel's eyes can't keep up with it.

FOUR. FIVE. SIX.

And done.

"That wasn't fair," Rachel huffs. "I wasn't ready." Ally ignores her and turns to me. This time I don't turn away fast enough.

"You wanna play?" she asks.

"Uh..." I look behind me to be sure it's me she's talking to.

"I'll go easy on you since you're new," she says. And that's all I need to get me up on my feet.

On my way to the ball, three boys I recognize from my class head straight for me. The two picking up the rear are shoving a rag doll of a kid toward me and laughing. Even floppy boy manages to giggle.

"Hey, you!" one of them calls to me and pushes the kid again. "He likes you!"

This makes the boys crack up and the rag doll blush.

I feel my cheeks flush red too, but it's not because I like

him or think he actually likes me or anything. I barely recognize him from the sea of gawking faces from when Mrs. Quakely introduced me to the class. The only reason I probably remember him at all is because he's Black. The only other Black kid besides me in our class, so naturally, the other boys want to pair us up. To them, we match. Like shoes.

"Beat it, Kenny," Ally says. "We're playing a game."

"Shut up, Ally!" the boy called Kenny hisses.

"Make me," she says, and without a hint of hesitation drops the ball and takes two steps forward.

"You've just got a bug up your butt 'cause your parents got a *divorce!*" Kenny taunts. But even though Ally's cheeks turn pink, she doesn't budge.

Kenny finally rolls his eyes, and he and his sidekick turn and walk off.

"Never mind them. They're just punks," Ally says to me, then turns to the third boy. "Marcus, you shouldn't let them push you around like that."

But Marcus only shrugs and runs off to the opposite end of the playground. To its big, empty field. Far from swings, handball courts, and bullies.

Ally sighs and turns back to me. "You ready?"

I nod, and as I do I feel a couple of sprinkles land on my face. The sky is pretty gray, but Mom didn't say anything about rain.

"You know how to play?" Ally asks, holding up the ball. I nod.

"I think so," I say, trying to hide my smile.

The sprinkles quickly become droplets, and then full-on rain, but by that time, Ally and I are neck and neck in what has fast become a real competition. A crowd has even gathered to watch.

"Okay, this is 6-6," she says. "The winner of this one wins the championship!" Her wild, wavy hair has gone flat, and I can feel my soaked braids hanging heavy at my ears. But before she can toss the ball up to start the next game, I hear a voice in the distance and see the crowd start running for our classroom. Mrs. Quakely is standing outside the door with a polka-dot umbrella, motioning for everyone to get inside and out of the rain. Ally sighs, grins at me, then drops the ball and runs for class.

"Next time!" she says. I give her a nod and a smile. That was fun. *Next time.* I'm already looking forward to it.

Back in the classroom, tucked in and cozy against the downpour, I've buried my face in a really good book for quiet reading time. My hand absently goes to stroke one of my braids...and I realize there's no braid there at all. The hair band that secured the end of it is gone. Probably swimming in a puddle on the playground. I move my hand across the top of my head. My hair is still damp from the rain, but it's drying rapidly now—and it seems the band from the other braid is swimming in that same puddle outside somewhere, because both braids have come completely loose, and my drying hair is rising UP and OUT.

I try to press it down, to make it lay flat, but I know better. The drier it gets, the bigger it's going to get. And there's no use braiding it again. It won't hold without clips or bands. In a class of straight- and wavy-haired kids, my hair is loud. It screams to be noticed, singled out. I'm already the new kid. I don't need another KICK ME sign on my back.

I'm doing my best to flatten my 'fro when Mrs. Quakely calls from the old upright piano in the corner. "Okay, sixth graders! Close those books and meet me for song time!" She claps her hands and smiles at the clock. Only twenty minutes of class left. Maybe my hair can behave just a little longer.

We gather around, on chairs and on the floor, circling Mrs. Quakely, who strikes up a bouncy tune on the piano.

"Rachel, be a fabulous young lady and hand out a song sheet to everyone," she says, motioning her wide chin to a stack of papers on top of the piano. When I get mine, I only have a moment to glance at the words before Mrs. Quakely begins.

"Join in!"

We're off to a clumsy start, but soon we pick up the melody and the words to what has to be *the* most ridiculously silly song I have ever heard, let alone sung along to. All about a billboard that's been torn to shreds by weather and now none of what it says makes sense. Or, rather, it makes the craziest kind of sense.

"Smoke Coca-Cola cigarettes, Drink Wrigley's Spearmint beer"???

Even though the song is beyond corny, Mrs. Quakely sits up very straight at the piano, pleasantly smiling throughout as though she were leading the church choir in Sunday service. And somehow that makes the song even funnier. In no time, the entire class has the giggles.

Mrs. Quakely does her best to guide us back.

"Keep it together, people. You're doing so well!"

We finally gather ourselves, and by the time we've laughed our way through two *more* crazy songs, I have forgotten all about my hair. All I can think of are my sore cheeks. It's been a while since I've laughed so hard. But when the bell rings and I'm pushing myself up from the rug, I'm reminded.

"Whoa!" Kenny is patting my head and I'm suddenly aware of how completely dry my hair is. How big and full it has become. "Please don't squeeze the Charmin!" he says.

Please don't squeeze the Charmin?

Ugh. It's the line from that stupid toilet paper commercial.

"Even more squeezably soft!" He scrunches a chunk of my hair. "It's so fluffy," he says, laughing.

Before I have a chance to say anything or to knock him away, more hands join in. Patting my hair. Grabbing handfuls. All of them laughing and chiming in with Kenny.

"Can I touch it?" a girl asks, her fingers already pushing through my kinks. Fists curling around it. More hands are squeezing, poking, exploring.

"It's like cotton candy!"

"Looks like a dandelion puff!"

"Okay—" I do my best to remind them that there's a person attached to my cotton top, but no one seems to hear me. Or maybe they just don't care.

I try to stand upright but can't do it with the crowd hovering over me.

"I'm gonna make a wish!" Kenny's sidekick Donald says, then proceeds to blow a spittle-laced stream of hot air at the side of my head.

"Quit it!" I hear myself shout.

"Please don't squeeze the Charmin!" Kenny sings again, and this time a couple of other kids sing along. Then, all at once, the voices stop. The hands are gone and it's only my arms shielding my head.

"What are you all up to? Go on! Get! Class dismissed!"
Mrs. Quakely commands as she lifts me from the floor by
my raised arms. "I'm ashamed of you," she barks at the dis-
persing crowd. Most hang their faces as they hurry off, but
a few share looks of amazement before they stroll away.
None take so much as a glance back at the petting zoo that
was my head.

Mrs. Quakely turns to me.

"You okay? Sorry about that, Stevie. I guess being
cooped up from the rain has turned everyone a little crazy."

I nod, but I don't think any of that had to do with the
rain.

Chapter Three

Hello?" I call into our house, but clearly no one's around. Mom's car isn't out on the street, and Dad is never here this time of day. Of all the days for no one to be here when I get home. I could really use a hug.

"Meow." It's my orange tabby, Elvis.

"Hey there, boy," I say, scooping him into my arms and climbing the stairs. "Wanna hear about my lame day?"

Once upstairs, I hit my parents' room. I think a little dress-up might be just the medicine I need after today.

The row of faceless Styrofoam heads on Mom's dresser, each topped with a fancy hairdo, offers up the different "me's" I can choose from.

There's the "Pixie." *"She's playful and edgy."*

There's the "Pageboy." Which *should* be called the

"Toadstool" since it looks like a mushroom sat on your head.

And then there's the "Ava." Shiny shoulder-length waves. Pure movie star. Named for possibly the most glamorous actress of the 1950s: Ava Gardner. Yes. This is what I need right now. It's gotta be Ava.

Getting my big 'fro to fit under Mom's wig cap is serious work, but after a good amount of shoving and sweating and an army of bobby pins, I manage to hide it all.

Once the wig's on, I enter Mom's closet of magic. Bold-patterned dresses, gold lamé blouses, and satin gloves can turn me into anyone I want. A beauty queen, a showgirl, Nefertiti.

My best friend, Jennifer, and I used to dress up in my mom's clothes all the time. We'd act out scenes from our favorite movies. Sometimes we'd even sit Mom down on the living room couch and put on full shows with props and everything.

My mom's maxi dresses with long skirts that sweep the floor when we walk are Jennifer's favorites.

"They make me feel like a princess," she always said. I prefer dressing up like the tough dames from the old movies. Bette Davis. Barbara Stanwyck.

I wonder how Jennifer's first day of school went. If she got kooky old Mr. Hutchinson like she'd hoped. Jennifer and I have been in the same class since the third grade, and before we moved across town this past summer, we lived across the street from each other, and I would see her every day. The last time I saw her was in swim class when she was hanging out with snooty old Trina Carlson and Melinda Whatshername. But I ducked out early on account of having failed to swim across the big pool and graduate to Fish. I chickened out. *It's eight feet deep!* Mrs. Salway was going to make me swim in the baby pool with all the little-kid Polliwogs. There was no way I was doing that.

But I never got to say goodbye to Jennifer.

I tried calling her after, but it seemed like she was never home, and then she went to England with her family for the last couple months of summer.

But it's fall now. She's got to be back and in school.

I should try her again.

"Hi, Lizzie. It's Stevie," I say when Jennifer's little sister answers the phone. "Is Jennifer there?"

Lizzie doesn't say anything to me, but I hear her drop the phone and call, "Jenny?"

I listen hard and think I can make out some voices far away from the phone, only I can't understand what they're saying. I wait for a long time and am starting to think that maybe Lizzie forgot about me when I hear rustling, and someone speaks into the phone.

"Hello? Who's this?" I recognize the voice of Jennifer's mom, Elaine, right away.

"Hi, Elaine. It's Stevie. Is Jennifer home?"

"Oh, hi, Stevie. Um..." She hesitates and then says, "Uh, no, dear. I'm sorry. Jen isn't home right now. How was your first day at your new school?"

"Oh, it was okay," I say. "Do you know when she'll be back?"

"I'm not sure. Sorry, Stevie."

"Well, can you tell her I called? Ask her to call me back?" I can hear kids squabbling.

"I sure can. Take care, Stevie. Tell your mom I said hello, okay?"

She hangs up before I say I will.

And I do my best to understand why Jennifer might not want to speak with me. Why she wouldn't come to the phone when I distinctly heard her yelling at her sister in the background.

I shimmy out of my corduroys and step into Mom's latest purchase: a sleeveless maxi with a skirt scattered in brilliant yellow sunflowers. I wrap the satin sash around my waist, then crisscross it in front of my chest and tie it behind my neck, creating my own design.

Once the wig and clothes are on, it's time for my face. Inky lines around my eyes, feathery lashes, rouged cheeks, and lips in shades of cherry.

We don't have money for real sapphires and diamonds,

but Mom's sparkling jewelry box overflows like pirate treasure. I clip on dangly earrings and wrap the long, beaded necklaces around and around my wrists until they are bejeweled cuffs. I find a necklace of gleaming red stones, lift it to my forehead, and secure the clasp behind my head. The garnet teardrop in its center creates a third eye.

I hop up on my parents' bed so I can see my full reflection in the mirror. As I stare at the dazzling beauty I've transformed into, I smile and push the memories of my first day of school firmly away.

Chapter Four

Friday, 3:30 p.m.

I have never been so happy for the weekend. While the first day of school was hands down the worst of the week, the following days weren't so much better. On Tuesday, Mom packed a liverwurst sandwich for my lunch.

"Yuck! What is *that*?" Kenny groaned.

"Looks like baby poop on white bread!" Donald said with a howl. "Gross!"

Before I knew it, kids from my class, and *other* classes, were standing around me, craning their necks for a better look.

"Disgusting!"

"I'm gonna throw up!"

"Are you really gonna *eat* that?"

The sandwich quickly made its way to the trash and I spent the rest of the day with my arms wrapped around my middle trying to muffle the growling of my angry, starving stomach.

Then, on Wednesday, Mercedes, the girl who sits next to me, offered to trade presidents with me.

"Want mine?" She held up her slip of paper.

"I don't think we can," I whispered.

"Sure we can," she said. "We haven't started writing our reports yet."

I leaned in to read Mrs. Quakely's pretty handwriting on the thin piece of paper.

John Quincy Adams

Son of the second president and one of the only presidents who didn't own slaves.

"Okay!" I said, scrambling to find John Tyler to hand him over.

But after lunch, while researching our subjects, Mrs. Quakely appeared over our desks, one hand on her hip and the other held out in front of her.

"Hand me your presidents," she said to both of us.

The rest of the class paused their pencils and pushed

their ears in a little closer to our desks. I heard a few shared whispers but couldn't make out what they were saying.

Mercedes and I handed over our papers, and while Mrs. Quakely read, I scanned the room. A dozen or so pairs of big, excited eyes shined with glee. Kenny even pointed at me and mouthed the word "busted!"

"I thought that I expressly said there's to be no swapping of subjects," said Mrs. Quakely, looking at Mercedes and then to me.

Without a second of hesitation, Mercedes pointed to me and said, "It was her idea! I was trying to help her since she's new."

I think the whole room could hear my jaw drop to the floor. I think my jaw is still there now.

On Thursday, I waited behind three other girls to play tetherball as Ally beat them one after another. I could hardly wait for my turn, my chance at the championship, when Rachel cut in front of me.

"Is it okay if I go next?" she asked, but then turned away and jumped into the next game before I could say anything. Halfway through the game the bell rang and I never had a chance to play.

I almost make it through today—the last day of the week—without any annoyance or humiliation. But as I'm walking home, snatching up wedding flowers and pretty yellow daisies from along the curb, creating the perfect bouquet, I hear:

"Please don't squeeze the Charmin!"

It comes from across the street. Kenny and Donald.

Ugh!

They laugh as they pass. A group of girls trail behind them, and a couple of them even join in with the boys, looking my way and snickering. Tetherball Ally is with them, but she doesn't snicker. She waves. I'll bet all the girls are going over to her house, where they'll make sandwiches and eat homemade cookies her mom made from scratch. They'll do each other's hair and play Parcheesi. They'll look at magazines and help each other with their homework.

I ignore them all and bury my face in my bouquet, pretending to be lost in its beautiful aroma. But these flowers don't have any smell. They only have ants. One starts to crawl up my nose and I quickly begin batting away at it. Frantically huffing and swatting at my nostrils. The laughter across the street gets even louder, and I take off for home.

Mom's car is parked in front of our apartment building, so I know she's inside, but I still let myself in with my key.

Mom gave it to me just after we moved in. She says I'm big enough now. But I wear it around my neck to be sure I don't lose it.

I follow the sound of Mom's voice into the kitchen, pulling my bouquet apart and sticking flowers in door-jambs and light sockets as I make my way to her. When I reach the kitchen, I see my aunt Mona seated at the table. She's draining the last of her grape punch from the glass and shaking ice cubes into her mouth. Spotting me in the entrance, her eyes smile wide, and I can hear her chomp down hard on the ice.

"Ooh! Baby girl!" she calls through a mouthful of crushed ice. Arms outstretched, she wiggles her fingers, directing me to come to her.

Mom's leaning against the counter by the sink, phone cradled in her shoulder. She nods a hello to me between "uh-huhs" and "oh nos." Even though Aunt Mona isn't technically on the phone, this is clearly a three-way conversation between Mom, her sister Mona, and her other sister, Florence. Mom and her sisters are tight. Especially Mom and Florence. When they talk, the world falls away and my mom is like a teenager again. They aren't twins, but they're only a year apart and might as well be. Ever since my uncle Lamont passed away last fall, they talk *every* day. Florence lives in a big ol' house all the way in Boston. Thousands of miles from Santa Monica. I thought living across town from Jennifer was bad. I can't imagine what it'd be like to have my best friend live clear across the country.

Aunt Mona is the oldest. She lives in Inglewood, which isn't that far away, so we get to see her often. She has really bad diabetes and sometimes has to go to the hospital. It even made her go blind once! So we help her out with grocery shopping and stuff. Mom says that anything we can do to make things a little easier for her makes a difference. I never mind one bit 'cause I'm crazy about Aunt Mona. And she's crazy about me. She loves nothing more than to smother me in kisses and butterscotch candies.

"Come here and give me some sugar!" she says as soon as she spots me. I get a tight squeeze and feel her silky cheek against mine. Mona has the softest skin in the world. "Sit, baby." I plop down on her thigh and answer her questions about school and new friends (or lack of) for a few minutes before I see the plate of *homemade cookies* on the counter. I turn to Mom and smile. Well, I may not be practicing braids on my friend's hair, but at least I've got cookies.

"Uh-huh," she says into the phone as she motions with her chin for me to take one. I take two. Mom walks to the chair across from us, the curly phone cord pulled tight across the center of the kitchen. As she leans back in her chair, long legs extended and ankles crossed, it's obvious she was once a model. She's so poised and elegant. That was back before she met my dad. Mostly modeling bras and swimsuits for catalogs. She graduated from the Barbizon School of Modeling.

"The only Black girl and still at the top of my class."

Mona says Mom could've been one of those Sears catalog models, that a big modeling agency expressed interest in her when she graduated from Barbizon, but that when she got married, she had to make a choice.

I'm too big to be propped up on Mona's lap like this. I feel like a ventriloquist's dummy. "I'm gonna get some milk. Want some?" I whisper to her as I pull away. Her face is still beaming at me as she shakes her head no.

"Well, at least she's back home safe and sound, Flo," Mom says into the phone, turning a concerned face to Mona. "Running away! How frightening. I am so sorry you had to go through that."

"You tell her Auntie Mona gonna come whoop that girl's behind if she keeps on with all that trouble," Mona calls to the receiver.

They must be talking about my cousin Naomi. Fifteen years old and "full of fight," according to Mona. She and her mom rarely used to argue, but now that her dad's gone, it's just the two of them in that house and they're always going at each other. Or at least, that's what I've overheard.

I take two more cookies, and my milk, and head to the living room. I'm on my knees in front of the TV changing the channels when my dad comes through the front door.

"Heya, kiddo!" He opens the coat closet and makes the usual small talk as he unloads his briefcase, jacket, and bundle of newspapers. Though he has a vending machine business these days with my uncle Owen, I've heard Mom complaining about how he spends most of his time at the local coffee shops reading the paper and drinking black coffee.

"Learn anything in school?"

"Nope."

"Teach that teacher of yours a thing or two?"

"Yep."

He appears from behind the closet door, chuckling.

"Good goin'," he says, then, spotting a daisy tucked into the closet's door hinge, he plucks it and sticks it behind his ear. "Pretty." He smiles and winks.

Just then, Mom walks Mona in from the kitchen.

"What? Who let *her* in here?" my dad teases.

"There he is!" Mona dances to him, then glances up at the clock. "Whatchoo doing home from work so early?"

"Early? I've been going since seven this morning!" he says.

"See! I *told* you you got yourself a good one!" Mona elbows Mom, then turns back to my dad. "Coop, I was just telling Kitty how you need to step in and help our Flo. That Naomi is about to run her into an early grave!"

"How am I supposed to help with that?" he says, laughing.

"You got an extra room," she says, gesturing upstairs where my dad's office was supposed to be. It was less like an office and more like the place where all the junk he collects from auctions went to die: typewriters missing ribbons, Xerox machines in need of plastic panels, telephones whose receivers don't match the phone. But now that he and Owen have found a warehouse downtown for the vending machines, Dad's been using *that* as his office. And Mom made him move all his junk there. Nobody's figured out what to do with that room since.

Mona continues, "And you'd be a father figure for her. She needs that right now."

"Father figure? Me?" He hoots. "Heya, Stevie! You think your pop could be a father figure?"

"You? Nah!" I say.

"What?" He pretends to be outraged and dives in to tickle my ribs.

"Okay, okay, funny guy," Mona says, sauntering over to him. "Gimme my kiss and I'll be outta here."

Dad leaps over the back of the couch to avoid her.

"A kiss? Help!"

"Get over here, you big chicken!" she says, chasing after him, but he darts up the stairs. She waves a dismissive hand his way. "Forget you, then!"

Mom's at the front door gathering Mona's purse and shaking her head at the two of them.

"I'm just going to run Mona home, then I'll be back, okay, pumpkin?" she says. "When I get back, I want all these flowers cleaned up. You got my house looking like some hippie commune!"

I nod and give my auntie a big squeeze.

"Don't you go getting all crazy on me like your daddy, you hear me?" Mona says, chuckling. "He's one piece of work."

Once Mona's gone, I run upstairs, grab the box full of cool stuff I've been collecting for my new clubhouse, and head down the balcony stairs to the tiny room under our new apartment. Jennifer and I used to have a clubhouse in the shed behind our old building. It took us a couple of weeks, but after we covered the walls in pictures we'd cut out of magazines and posters from *Tiger Beat* of our favorite actors, it became a really cool hangout. Jennifer's mom gave us a couple of beanbag chairs and we kept a ton of board games there. It was the best.

I scoped the new room out as soon as we moved in. The door to it looks like something from *Charlie and the Chocolate Factory*. And while it's tall enough for *me* to walk through without a problem, a grown-up would have to duck to enter. Inside, it's super dusty and cobwebs creep all along the beams of the short ceiling, but none of that bothers me. There's a flashlight just inside the door. I turn it on and set it upside down on a ledge so the whole room is lit. There aren't any windows so without the flashlight it's pitch-black and kinda scary. Off to one side, there's a tunnel that leads to the underside of all five of the building's apartments. Electricians and plumbers have to climb through there if there's a problem with a circuit or the hot water. Other than that, no one ever comes down here.

I'm going to clean this place up, write a big list of rules, and have a secret pass code to enter.

Elvis slinks in through the little door and hops up into the tiny tunnel.

"Oh no! No you don't!" I grab ahold of him before he can go exploring.

I hold the cat with one arm while I rummage through the box with the other. There's a large jar of Elmer's glue, the God's eye I made last year, a few long stretches of lace from Mom's sewing box that I don't think she'll miss. . . .

I'm not sure what I'm going to do with any of this stuff. Maybe make a design on a wall? Like a cool mural?

Mom would probably love it if I did a black-and-white movies club. She loves how beautiful those old films look. The glamour of the old stars. I could fill the walls with pictures from old movies. That'd be cool.

But I think that maybe I should just wait for Jennifer to help me figure it out. After all, the club's going to be both of ours. At least I hope so.

I haven't been back up in my room long when there's a knock on my door, quickly followed by Dad throwing it open.

"You've gotta wait until I say come in!" I say, and close the door on him.

"Oh, okay," I hear him mumble in the hall, then . . .

Knock knock.

"Who is it?" I ask.

"It's the big bad wolf. May I come in?"

"Yes, wolfman. You may enter," I say. Dad slowly opens the door, revealing a silly grin.

"Did I do good?" he asks.

"Much better. Thank you. What's up?" I ask. Dad almost never comes to my room, so I know he must have a good reason.

"Throw something pretty on, Stevie. We're hitting the town!"

My parents go out a lot. At least three nights a week, Mom will slip into one of her chicest dresses, Dad will shine up his best shoes, and they'll go somewhere super fancy. And, while it doesn't happen often, every now and then *I* get to go, too!

I haven't said much to Dad about my new school. Seems like I've hardly seen him. But I'm guessing Mom must've told him about my bummer of a week.

"Really?"

"You betcha, kiddo! You tackled your first week at a new school. I think that's cause for celebration," he says. "I'm proud of you."

I can't help but smile. He's right. I battled through, and even though it was hard, I beat that first week. As much as it tried, it didn't destroy me.

As we approach the restaurant, a brass lion's head looks down on us from up high above a huge shellacked door. A burly man in a tuxedo nods and steps to the side to allow us in. As I pass by, I look up at him and he gives me a wink.

A bright-eyed hostess in all black, hair pulled tight from her face, greets us.

"Good evening. Three?" she chirps.

Before my parents can answer, a walrus in a suit, with a protruding belly, appears and thrusts a hand into my dad's, nodding and smiling.

"Welcome, welcome! So good to see you back, Mr. Morrison."

"Good to see *you*, Francesco," Dad says, and smiles back.

My dad is real good at making friends with the guys in tuxedos at the front of the restaurants. With everyone, really. He seems to remember each of their names and all about their aunt with the kidney problem, or the teenager leaving for college. He makes them laugh and they're always happy to see him when we come back.

The man gestures toward my mom, shaking his head and saying over and over, "Bellissima, bellissima," before finally taking her hand, kissing it, and then nodding to my father with approval.

Mom blushes a little, smiling. With every "bellissima" she utters a small "thank you."

It isn't long before the walrus has grabbed an inch of my cheek between his fat fingers and given it a shake.

The man turns to the hostess and says something into

her ear, low and impossible for us to hear, and then flashes his bright teeth at us.

"Welcome, welcome," he says again, and disappears.

The hostess lifts three menus from her stand.

"Please follow me." She pushes aside the velvet curtain to reveal a dark but lively room. Clouds of smoke from cigarettes, cigars, and sweet-smelling pipes hang in the air, their aroma mingled with marinara sauce. My parents like Italian places.

There's music and everyone's dressed up. I feel like we're dead in the middle of one of Mom's favorite black-and-white movies. Like any minute now some glossy Hollywood actress will come around the corner in a full-length-sequins gown.

Dad can't hide his satisfied grin as the other customers lift their heads from their fancy cocktails. They all want a better look at my mom.

Six-foot-two in her heels, she bats her lashes as her silky waves dust her chestnut shoulders. Without even trying, Mom has all the glamour of a star like Rita Hayworth or Gene Tierney. But even though Mom says she loves her maxi dresses with their skirts that sweep the floor like those of the movie stars, she *always* wears a mini when she goes out to dinner with my dad.

"You've got great legs," I've heard him say. "Why would you want to hide them?"

It isn't until we're just approaching our table that I realize I only see *one* other Black person in the place. A pencil of a man in a white suit loading finished dinner plates onto a wide, round tray.

Everyone else is white.

My dad is white, too. Welsh and Scottish. He's five-foot-seven if he's lucky, and isn't a bad-looking man, but his crisp white shirt and polished shoes can't magically make him handsome. His black hair is slicked back behind thick sideburns. His thick-rimmed glasses and very large nose form the centerpiece of his face.

Together, my parents make quite an entrance anywhere they go.

We settle into a dark red booth with brass button trim. Mom's "special" perfume, Chanel No. 5, sweetens up the little vinyl corner that still smells faintly of spilled liquor from what must've been a good time the night before. The booth has a perfect view of the stage and everyone in the place. It's also the perfect spot to claim if you want to be *seen*. Looking at Dad's grin as he scopes out the crowd, I'm guessing *that's* why we're seated here.

He orders a whiskey neat.

Mom, a glass of sherry.

I get my favorite: a Shirley Temple with three cherries.

Across the room, on a small, raised platform, a man in

a slim-fitting tux, cigarette dangling from his lips, taps on the keys of a black baby grand piano while a red-haired singer in green silk sways.

As she studies the menu, Mom's shoulders do a little shimmy to the music. Dad leans back and sips his drink, checks out the room.

"What'll it be, Stevie?"

The menu is tall with black script writing. It's hard to make out all the letters.

"I don't know," I say.

I have the menu up close to my face, squinting and trying to read my choices, when Dad calls the waiter over. He's got a head like a light bulb, a small notepad and pencil in his hands.

"Good evening," he says and nods to each of us. "Allow me to tell you tonight's specials." With a heavy Italian accent, he rattles off the night's special foods, all Italian words. Mom leans forward as she listens, smiling and nodding. But I can't understand a thing. As soon as the waiter is finished, he turns to my mother and grins. "Signora?"

"Yes," she says. She lifts her menu and attempts to pronounce her selection, a pretty, red fingertip underlining each syllable as she begins, but before she can finish, Dad breaks in.

"You loved the eggplant parmesan last time. Remember?" He nods to her.

"I did...," she says.

Dad turns to the waiter. "She'll have the eggplant parmesan," he says.

Mom looks surprised, but when the waiter turns to her, she doesn't say anything. Simply nods.

"Excellent choice," he says, and makes a note.

"I'll have the steak," Dad says. "Can you make sure it's cooked well but not dry?" The man nods and writes. "And we'll have the spinach and an order of garlic bread for the table."

"And for la bambina?" he asks my dad as he nods toward me.

I still can't make out the fancy letters on the menu, but I answer for myself all the same.

"I'll have the spaghetti."

The man makes a note, smiles at me, takes our menus, and scurries away.

Dad is enjoying the flame-topped singer.

"She's pretty good!"

Mom lifts her drink and turns to me. I lift my Shirley Temple and we clink glasses. As soon as Mom takes a sip, her eye catches something.

"Coop!" She shakes Dad's wrist. "It's Don Adams!"

Seated in a booth across the room is the actor who played bumbling secret agent Maxwell Smart on TV. It's one of the few shows my dad watched with us. I think it's because before he met my mom, he briefly worked for the CIA. Mom says he was a kind of spy. And every now and then I still catch him doing stuff from his spy days. Just last week, a man called the house asking for someone named Bob.

"I'm sorry, there's no one here named Bob," I said, and started to hang up. My dad was fast at my side, snatching the phone away from me. He gestured for me to beat it.

My dad's name is Cooper.

Dad starts shuffling around under the table and in no time he's got his shoe up to his ear, just like the Maxwell Smart character does with his shoe phone. He pretends to talk into it, laughing and pointing at the actor, who sees him from across the room and offers up a friendly smile. I'm guessing he's seen that one before. But Dad doesn't care. I think he just loves that it makes Mom laugh.

"So, Stevie," Dad begins as he tries to squeeze his shoe back on. "We wanted to talk to you about something."

Oh no. Did they finally find out I cut swim class last summer?

"Am I in trouble?"

"No, no, no," Mom says, and then nods at me to look back at Dad. She seems to be holding her breath.

"Well, your mom and I have been talking about it and

43

we think it'd be a good idea for your cousin to come stay with us for a little while."

My cousin? What *cousin*?

"Naomi," Mom says, reading my mind. "Aunt Flo's little girl."

Naomi. Right. The one whose dad died recently. The one who's been fighting with her mom all the time. The one who's been getting into trouble. The one who *ran away*. The one who would probably like nothing better than to be sent clear across the country to live with a bunch of relatives she hardly even knows! Brilliant idea! Why didn't *I* think of it?

"Your aunt Flo could use a break, Stevie. And I'll bet it'll be good for Naomi, too," says Dad.

"And think about it, it'll be a little like having a big sister," Mom says.

"Didn't she run away?" I ask.

I ran away once when I was six. Threw Rose Marie, my flowered elephant, and my pajamas into my mom's makeup case and stormed out of the house. My mom didn't even try to stop me. Just watched me go. I'd gone about three blocks—felt like I'd traveled miles at the time—when it started raining. I ran back home drenched and crying. I went up to my room while Mom ran me a warm bath.

Neither one of us said another word about it. But I was *six*. I have a feeling this is different.

"She did. She's fine now, though—"

"That's just crazy," Dad says, and shakes his head. "Where the hell did she go?"

"Language," Mom scolds. "Some older friends—and a boy, I think—live in an apartment in Roxbury. Not far, it's just that Flo had no idea where she was. They'd had a fight."

"How'd they find her?" I ask. "Did she go back on her own?"

"A friend saw her. Convinced her to call home," Mom says, then lets out a heavy sigh. "She's just got herself mixed up with a crowd that Flo's not crazy about. Always getting in trouble with the police. Not *Naomi* yet. She's a good kid. Very bright."

"Teenage girls!" Dad laughs. "Just you wait!" He points to Mom, then to me, winks, and laughs.

"Why are you pointing at me? I'm not running away!" I say.

"Ha!" he says, still laughing. "We'll see!"

Just then, the Black man in the white suit arrives with our food.

"Thank you," Mom says to him as he places the eggplant

parmesan in front of her. He smiles but doesn't meet her eyes.

Mom turns to Dad. "Did you know Flo and Lamont were high school sweethearts? Did you know that?"

Dad nods as he begins sawing his steak.

"I think I remember him telling me that," he says, and they both get quiet. Then Dad chuckles to himself. "You remember Lamont's Oldsmobile?"

Mom laughs and says, "I do!"

I twirl my spaghetti around and around my fork, but I can't manage more than two bites. I don't know if it's the suddenness of learning that my cousin's moving in or if it was all the garlic bread.

"Oh, Stevie," Mom says. "You can do better than that."

"I'm so stuffed," I moan.

As my parents order wine and drink and eat and drink some more, my eyelids get heavy. At first it's just small wafts of drowsiness, but soon I'm in a battle with myself to sit upright.

"Mom, I'm so tired," I tell her. "I can't keep my eyes open."

"Lie down, kiddo," Dad says. "Go ahead." My mom gives a look around the room before agreeing with my dad.

"Sure, sweetheart. I guess it's okay."

Even though the vinyl seat is cold and sticks to my cheek, I'm relieved to be able to close my eyes and drift.

The restaurant's music pulses through my dreams and I'm twirling and spinning and laughing. At one point, my eyes open and my parents aren't in the booth with me anymore. Panic jolts me upright and I see that the room has changed. The lights have dimmed even more. The center of the room is filled with bodies now. Everybody is dancing. Deep in the thick of the crowd, I spot my mom and dad. They're dancing, too. My mom twirling and spinning and laughing.

Chapter Five

And just like that, my cousin Naomi is coming to stay with us. At first, Mom and Dad seemed to be trying the idea on like a winter coat. I'd overhear them running through scenarios involving her going to school. *Where will she go? Can she walk there? And home? How do we keep her busy? Are there clubs? Does she have hobbies?*

Mom really liked the idea of Naomi helping her out around the house and watching after me sometimes. And Dad seemed to think my having an older "companion" wasn't such a bad thing.

But *me*? Well, no one ever asked *me* for *my* opinion. Look, I know I'm a kid and all, and I never get a say in anything, but you'd think they'd at least *ask* me what I thought about it.

"I think it's exciting, don't you? It'll be like having a big sister!" Mom kept saying.

A big sister? Why does everyone just assume I even *want* a big sister? Since when was that the coolest thing in the world? I don't need an older sister bossing me around, hogging the bathroom, choosing what ice cream we'll eat or what shows we'll watch. I like being an only child. I don't have to share the television. When Mom gets ice cream or doughnuts, she asks me what *I* want. *My* choice. I get Saturdays with my mom. *My* mom. I don't have to share those days *or my mom*, for that matter. No, I'm perfectly happy being an only child, thank you very much.

At lunch, perched atop the monkey bars or alone at the back of the cafeteria, I'd imagine what it might be like having Naomi there. Whenever I could, I watched the other kids with big brothers or sisters. Studied how they acted together. If they liked each other and if older girls were nice to girls my age or not. Mostly, they didn't seem to say much to one another. Each in their own world, even when they were walking for long stretches side by side. Except for Kim's big sister, who dropped her off at the gate one day screaming at her and leaving her in tears. Oh, man. I never even thought of that. What if Naomi is *mean*? Or what if she's not happy living with us? Just what makes everyone think she's going to be all smiles and sunshine? Who says she's even interested in being "Big Sis" to some kid she doesn't even know?

I went through *all* the photo albums and finally found *one* photo of Naomi and me together. I was a baby, probably one year old, and she must've been about five. In the photo she's desperately trying to keep me—the fat, squirming baby—from falling out of her lap and does not look happy about it.

On our way to the airport, Mom's rambling on and on about Naomi's arrival, barely taking a second to breathe between thoughts.

"We'll have to drop by Lucky's later so Naomi can pick out the things she likes to eat. It's not going to be like home, but I'd like it to be as comfortable and easy for her as possible. Maybe we can all help her decorate her room. I wish we knew another girl her age. I think that girl in apartment four is already in college."

Clearly she's pretty nervous about this whole thing, too.

I stay quiet, still trying to get used to the idea, but I don't know what to expect. All anyone's really told me about Naomi is that she's here because she's been getting into trouble and fighting with her mom. I guess they think that it's all going to change once she's here. Well, maybe. But have they ever thought that it might even get worse? That she'll be so mad that she got sent away that she'll go crazy on all of us? No! No one ever even considered *that* possibility. Great!

The airport is massive. So many people rushing. I hold on to Mom's arm and do my best to keep up with her quick pace. We walk for what seems like forever before we finally reach the gate and join the large crowd that's already there waiting. Loads of people file out of the plane. All shapes and sizes. Young parents trying to keep track of excited toddlers, carefree couples on vacation; there's a man with a dog in a basket; an elderly woman with a cane is placed in a wheelchair....As I study all of them, looking for my cousin, I realize that I don't really know what she looks like. The only pictures I've seen are of her when she was younger than I am. We haven't even visited Boston since I was a baby. Mom has brought up going to Dad a few times, but he always says, "No way. It's too expensive."

There aren't a lot of kids coming off the plane, and the ones I do see seem to be with their parents. But Naomi is flying all by herself, so I guess that'll make it easier to spot her. And there aren't a whole lot of Black people coming off the plane, either, so I guess that'll make it easier, too.

Suddenly my mom spots her. "Oh, there she is!" Mom waves her arm high.

A figure wearing skintight bell bottoms and a polyester top tied at the belly button comes into view. My cousin,

Naomi, emerges and I have to stick my eyes back in their sockets. She's got that Coke-bottle figure I've heard people talk about. The top button of her blouse is holding on to its buttonhole for dear life (I think it's about to lose the battle). She strolls over to us effortlessly in three-inch suede platform sandals. A floppy cap tilts to one side.

Is that what fifteen looks like? Is that what *I'll* look like in a few years?

She could be a *Soul Train* dancer.

Naomi catches me gawking at her and blows a big pink bubble.

"Look at you!" Mom says, her eyes wide, taking in Naomi's tight-fitting ensemble. Her grown-woman body. I don't think this was quite what she was expecting, either. Regardless of what she's thinking, she throws her arms around her niece.

"Hi, Aunt Kitty." Naomi's voice comes out singsongy as my mom squeezes and rocks her. As soon as Mom releases her, Naomi turns to me. I don't know what to say to her. I really hope I'm not expected to show her around or anything. Heck, are we going to have to play together? Everyone talked about her like she was a kid, but... she looks like a woman to me.

"What's up, cuz?" She tugs on one of my braids like we've known each other all our lives and blows another bubble.

The whole way home, Mom grills Naomi about her old school and her friends and what she likes to do. She tells her about Santa Monica and Elvis the cat.

"I forgot to even ask if you were allergic!"

"I'm not. I like cats. We used to have a cat."

"And I should probably warn you about your uncle Coop," Mom starts.

"Warn me?" asks Naomi, laughing.

Warn her? What's she talking about? What is there about my dad she'd need to *warn* her about?

"No, no. I shouldn't have put it like that. He's not so bad. It's just. Well, did you know he used to work for the CIA?"

I smile. Just hearing it out loud sounds pretty impressive. I mean, how many people do you know who worked for the CIA?

"Are you kidding?" Naomi sits up straight in her seat, turns to face Mom. "That agency's as crooked as they come!"

"*Crooked?*" I say, and leap forward in my seat, first looking at Naomi and then quickly to Mom for some sort of response.

"Well," she says, "it was a long time ago. And the agency isn't exactly what people think it is. And I certainly don't think *Coop* was ever 'crooked,'" she says firmly.

"Yeah. I'm sure it's all exaggerated," Naomi says. But as she turns to look out the window, her smirk in the side-view mirror tells me she's not convinced.

"Sure," says Mom. "But anyway, those were his glory days. He's proud of the work he did and, well...sometimes he still behaves like he's on a mission."

"He stacked pots and pans up near the front door once so if a burglar came in the night, we'd hear him," I add from my seat in back.

"Well, *that* may not have been a standard CIA procedure," Mom says with a laugh.

"But it works!" I say. "He knows loads of spy tricks."

Naomi chuckles at this. "So I take it he's a bit of a snoop?"

"Well, I wouldn't say that," says Mom, catching my scowl in the back seat. "But he does like to ask a lot of questions. Once a spy, always a spy, I guess. But he's harmless."

"That's funny." Naomi shakes her head and goes back to taking in the scenery. "It's so pretty here." Her eyes widen as she soaks up the blue skies and lush green that my mom always tells me I take for granted. Naomi pulls off her hat and fusses with her pressed curls a moment before she cranks the window open and leans her head out. From the back seat, I can see her smiling face in the side-view mirror.

Mom turns to me and grins.

I roll down my window to let the ocean breeze blow through me like Naomi is doing when I spot a huge crowd of people crossing the intersection just in front of us.

"Mom, look!" I jump forward and point. They're all walking together in one big group, right in the middle of the street. Some carry large hand-painted signs saying things like POWER TO THE PEOPLE and BLACK IS BEAUTIFUL! Those who don't have signs raise a fist to the sky. At the front of the group, a man shouts into a megaphone, and every time he does, the crowd repeats what he says.

> *"An attack against one is an attack against all!"*

"Is it some kind of parade?" I ask.

"It's a protest march," Naomi says, her eyes fixed on the sea of bodies walking in rhythm together.

"What are they holding their fists up like that for?" I ask.

"It symbolizes Black Power. And it means we will fight against those who would try to keep us down." Naomi's on the edge of her seat watching.

"I wish they wouldn't hold up traffic like this," Mom grumbles. As she turns to look out the side window, Naomi faces her.

"It's only for a couple minutes, but it gets people's attention, right? I think it's a good way of alerting people to the fight," she says.

"Well, I don't know about all that," Mom says, shaking her head. "*I* think it's inconsiderate."

When we get home, Mom pulls into the driveway and I see my uncle Owen's van parked across the street. It's almost a perfect match for my dad's white van, only Owen's has two little windows in the back and he *lives* in it all year-round! He doesn't have a job he has to go to, just works with my dad leasing and selling vending machines. "I have the freedom to follow the weather," he says. In the summer, he heads up north to Montana, where he and my dad are from, and as soon as it starts to get colder, he comes down to Southern California. I can't imagine what it'd be like to live in a van, but it is pretty cool that he comes and goes as he pleases.

"Stevie, dear, go tell Owen and your dad we need a hand."

Owen is a big ol' grizzly bear of a man. Burly and cuddly. He's got round, ruddy cheeks and a nose just as pink. His chin is rough as sandpaper. I swear whenever I hug him I come away with a rash on my face that lasts the rest of the day. He's eighteen years older than my dad. Oldest of four but the only one of Dad's siblings I've ever met. His sisters live in other states and have never come to visit. I mentioned our going up to visit them. I'd love to meet my other cousins. But my dad shut it down and we never talked about it again. Seemed like a sore subject.

"Uncle Owen!" I call as I enter the living room. On Saturdays, Owen and my dad play cards.

Owen turns from the card table and beams. "Now there's the prettiest little girl on God's green earth!" He makes his way to me and gives me one of his big bear hugs. I wrap my arms around his wide middle and give him a squeeze. Then I turn to my dad.

"Naomi's here! She's out in the car with Mom. We need some help with her things."

Unlike Mom, Dad makes no effort to hide his surprise at how much Naomi's grown up.

"What did this woman do with my sweet niece?" he asks my mom, pointing to Naomi and looking over her shoulder and behind the car door.

"It's me, Uncle Coop!" she says, swatting him and laughing.

"Ouch!" Dad says, cowering and turning to Owen. "This lady is strong!" Naomi laughs and swats him again, and this time, my dad lifts her up by the legs and over his back.

"You want me to toss you in the ocean?" he asks as he marches away. "It's not that far."

After protests and pleas to be put down, he finally marches back to the car, sets her down, and runs for cover behind my mom before she can hit him again.

"Don't you worry, young lady," says Owen. "I'll keep that crazy fella away from you. I'm Owen, the knucklehead's brother."

"Hi, Owen," Naomi says with a smile as she smooths her clothes and hair and puts her hat back on.

My dad and Owen take Naomi's suitcase and one large cardboard box, sealed with blue tape, upstairs to her new room. "Where you want this, young lady?" Owen's carrying the box now and it looks heavy, even for him. He leans it against the doorframe for support, face red and dripping like a Popsicle.

"Oh, anywhere is fine," Naomi says. She waves a limp hand through the air, then points to the bed. "Thanks." They deposit her suitcase and the box, side by side, on the bed. Dad gives me a "boy, was that heavy!" face and a wink before he and Owen head out.

"We'll be right downstairs. Don't hesitate to call if you need us, Naomi," he says.

Mom gestures around at the empty room. "We'll liven it up with pictures and things, okay? Just get yourself settled in—the bathroom's next door if you need to freshen up—and we'll give your mom a ring in a little bit to let her know you're in safe and sound. Okay?" Mom plants a big kiss on her hat.

"Thanks!" Naomi says, eyeing the walls, the carpet, the pink chenille bedcover. I wonder what her room in Boston was like. I know she lived in a whole house, not just an apartment. I'll bet it was a big room.

I hang back in the hall after they've all left, just out of Naomi's eyesight, watching her through a crack in the door.

Once everyone's gone, she kicks her platforms off, pulls her hat free, and scratches at her scalp.

The room is an empty shell. It feels cold and lonely even from out here in the hall.

Naomi walks around the room dragging her fingers along the bare, white walls, then stops at the window and stares out at Santa Monica. I know I can only see the back of her head, but still, she seems so...sad.

After a moment, she walks deliberately from the window, goes to the large box, and tears it open. She tosses out some sweaters, a couple heavy coats. I'm thinking maybe her mom didn't tell her about the Southern California sunshine. Finally, after she's littered the bed with clothes, she reaches deep into the box and pulls out a portable record player. Cool! She holds it tight to her chest and scans the room. Searches every inch of wall until her eyes land on a space just to the right of the bed. She goes and sets the record player on the floor, plugs it in, then goes back to the box and rustles about inside. I can't see what she's looking at but it makes her smile. When she straightens up, she's holding record albums. A stack of them. We only have four in the whole house: *Herb Alpert & The Tijuana Brass*, *Burl Ives Christmas Album*, *The Supremes*, and some yodeling lady.

Naomi leans them against the wall near the record player and flips through a few before landing on her choice. Her eyes linger on the cover image awhile before she shakes the album from its jacket, her fingers cranking the sound up before the singer even begins. Horns whine through the tiny speakers and the deep booming sends Naomi's head bobbing. A man's voice joins in with the instrumentals, his singing full of longing and pain. He growls and moans. At one point, he even screams. Naomi tosses the record jacket onto the bed. Eyes closed, arms stretched wide, fingers snapping, hips and head swaying.

"Naomi!"

My mom calling from downstairs breaks the spell.

I quickly duck back down the hall and into my room before Naomi can catch me spying.

She runs down the hall, past my room, and shouts back, "Yes, Aunt Kitty?"

"Come down. I have some lunch for you! Tell Stevie she can come down, too, if she's still hungry. We're going to give your mom a call." Then, "And please turn the music down a bit."

With lightning speed, I'm on my bed, pretending to be reading a book when Naomi sticks her head in my room.

"There's food downstairs if you're hungry. I'm about to get some," she says.

She's being nice to me. The way big kids are nice to little kids. Kinda like a babysitter. Like she has to be.

"Oh, that's okay," I say. "I already ate." I grin wide but she just nods and turns for her room. I hear her lift the needle from the record and run down the hall and stairs. I wait until I'm sure she's all the way in the kitchen talking to my mom. Their voices are so far away I can only make out the faint murmur of them, but it's enough to let me know the coast is clear. I toss the book on the bed and go into Naomi's room.

It feels even more cold and hollow from inside.

There's still stuff in the big box. Posters rolled into tubes and bound by rubber bands, all of them crushed by the heavier objects. Framed photos; one of Naomi with her mom and dad. They're in the woods and Naomi is wearing shorts and striped tube socks, sitting on a rock and smiling. Her parents stand on either side of her and lean in for the photo. Her dad is laughing, head thrown back and eyes closed. Her mom looks like a version of my mom. One that wears pants, a barely there smile, and no makeup.

Beneath a few worn paperbacks, I spot the jackpot—a diary! With its beautiful cover of pale blue and a gold peacock on the front, it's *got* to be a diary! A gold lock binds it shut. With both hands I feel around the bottom of the box for the small metal key, but I can't feel or see any such thing. She probably has it hidden somewhere.

I spot the album cover of the record she put on the bed, and the man on the front smiles sweetly up at me. The smile of a little boy up to no good. But I smile back. I like his face.

I count twelve albums on the floor near the record player. One in particular catches my eye. The band, all the colors of the rainbow, are all laughing together. They're having the best time ever. The one girl in the group—clearly the lead singer—is in the middle of them all and she's laughing the hardest. Her hair is bigger than *mine*! On the back of the album is a picture of just her wearing the same jeans and T-shirt. She rolls around on a bed thrusting her bare foot into the camera. She hasn't a care in the world. She's happy and free.

I want to play the first song of the record before Naomi

comes back, but I hear my mom and Naomi at the bottom of the stairs. No, they're moving *up* the stairs. Getting closer, fast! I hold the record tight to my chest, quickly tiptoe down the hall to my room, and tuck it under my mattress.

Chapter Six

At dinner, I spend the whole time worrying about whether Naomi has noticed the album is gone. But she doesn't seem to have. Mom and Dad ask Naomi what she thinks of Santa Monica, is there anything she needs, how she likes her room.

"It's perfect. Thank you," she says. "I brought some things from home to put on the walls and stuff. Make it my own, you know?"

"Let us know if you want any help or anything," Mom says. "There's Scotch tape in that top drawer, and I think you'll find thumbtacks in there, too."

"Santa Monica's a far cry from Boston," says my dad. "You won't need to bundle up like you're used to."

"Yes! That'll be so nice," she says.

"Tomorrow, I'll drive you by your new school so you can get a look at it before next week," Mom says. Naomi's lucky. Mom says since she needs a little time to get used to her new home, she gets to have the *whole* week off!

"Cool. Thanks," she says, and then turns to me. "Where's your school, Stevie?"

"Oh, I go to Walt Whitman now," I say.

"You just started going there?" Naomi asks, twisting the clasp of her necklace to the back of her neck and holding it there a moment, closing her eyes, and making a silent wish. I do that, too, when my necklace clasp floats to the front. When Naomi's finished wishing, the charm on the end of her necklace falls back onto her chest. A small gold key. Ah! It's *got* to be the key to her diary!

"Yeah, when we moved over the summer I had to switch," I say with a shrug. "It's all right, I guess."

Mom chimes in, "Stevie hasn't really found a group of friends there yet."

"Well, I guess we're both in the same boat, then, huh?" Naomi says.

I nod.

"You need to find some kids that are into the same stuff you're into," she says.

Easy to *say*! How am I supposed to do *that*?

"Oh...I don't know...I like roller-skating," I say.

"Really? That's so cool! Ever watch *Roller Derby* on TV?" she asks.

"Yes! I love *Roller Derby*!" I say, then point to my dad, who's been reading from the newspaper in his lap in between bites. "But Dad always makes me turn it off."

He looks up. "What? Oh, that roller-skating stuff? Bah! They think they're guys!" He swats a hand at the air.

"Guys?" Naomi turns to my dad. "What do you mean? Uncle Coop, you don't think women should play sports or something?"

Dad looks up from his paper and laughs. "I don't have any problem with women playing sports. Of course not. But those roller gals are shoving each other and... knocking each other down. Women shouldn't behave like that!"

Naomi shakes her head and looks at my mom, but Mom shrugs, silent. Loads a forkful of food into her mouth. Naomi frowns.

Dad continues, "I think there are some very skilled female tennis players and swimmers."

"But you said Billie Jean King was trying to be a man when she played against that guy," I butt in, reminding him. "That Battle of the Sexes, or whatever."

"Well, that's because she was playing *against* a man, as if she could *play* like a man," he scoffs.

"But she beat his behind!" says Naomi, laughing. "What do you say to that?"

Dad gives a chuckle, too, and shakes his head to himself before finally saying, "You don't want to hear what I think."

"Tell me," says Naomi, grinning and sitting back in her chair. Mom stands and clears the table, saying nothing. But I see her shoot a look at Dad, which he ignores.

"Me too. I wanna hear," I say.

When we watched that match, Dad left the room after it seemed pretty clear Billie Jean King was gonna whoop the guy. Huffed off. He's got a smile on his face now, though.

"Well, you two might be too young and naive to see it or understand it, but some people will do all sorts of things for ratings." Dad turns to Mom at the sink, running dishes under the water. "Isn't that right, Kitty?"

Mom shrugs and speaks over her shoulder. "Well, I guess they will sometimes...yes."

"You mean to tell me you think that her beating him was fake? Staged? Are you serious?" Naomi looks like she can't believe her ears. "Did you watch, Aunt Kitty? What did *you* think?"

"Well, I—" Mom starts.

"Look," Dad interrupts. "There's simply no way that a woman can beat a man."

Naomi's eyes widen. "Wow." She shakes her head and turns to Mom again. "You seriously thought it was fake?"

Dad quickly pipes in, "We all watched it together, and I think I can speak for the adults when I say that it was clearly a publicity stunt. Plain and simple."

"Mom?" I'm hoping she'll speak up. Dad thinks she feels the same way he does, but I'm not so sure. Still, when Naomi gets back into it with Dad, Mom just turns toward the sink.

"Honestly? You just can't believe that it's possible for a woman—an athlete like Billie Jean—to win a match with that old male chauvinist pig has-been?" Naomi shakes her head and turns to my mom again for some sort of backup that doesn't come. "But you saw it with your own eyes!"

"I saw the whole thing," I say, nodding.

"And did you think it was fake, Stevie?" she asks me.

"No! She kicked his male chauvinist pig butt!" I say. I'm not *exactly* sure what a "male chauvinist pig" is, but I like the sound of it.

"Sister, I'm with you on that," she says, shaking her head.

"Well, you're both still kids. One day you'll understand," Dad says, standing. He goes to Mom and kisses her cheek. "Thanks for the delicious meal, Kitty. I have to run out. Need to check on some machines that should've arrived this afternoon. It's really good to have you here, Naomi. Let us know if you need anything."

"Call to check in with me," Mom says.

"Will do."

And with that, he's gone.

Naomi shoots me a look that says she still can't believe my dad. When Mom finally joins us at the table, Naomi asks, "Aunt Kitty? Is Uncle Coop...a bit of a chauvinist?"

"Oh, I wouldn't go that far—"

"Yes!" I pipe in.

"Oh, Stevie, you don't even know what that means," she says, and before I can tell her that I think I do, she continues, "He's just old-fashioned. And you have to remember, a lot has changed since he came up. It's not always so easy for people to just...change."

After dinner, I sit on my bed and study the wild-haired singer with the bare feet. I look at her name on the cover.

Chaka Khan.

What kind of name is that? And why didn't she dress up for the photo shoot? It's an album cover. Aren't you supposed to wear your best clothes? Fix your hair? Put some shoes on?

But as I study the photo, with her sticking her toe right in my face, I can't help but get lost in that smile.

Chapter Seven

From the top of the monkey bars, I can see all the goings-on of the playground: Ally whipping everyone at tetherball. Kenny and Donald terrorizing Marcus and whoever else they please. Mrs. Quakely running through the halls in her heels, trying to get back to class before recess is over. It's my own private observation deck and I'm captain. And when I'm up here, no one can stick their grubby fingers in my hair or call me names.

Honestly, though, I've been dying to play tetherball with Ally again. And I can tell she wants another match, too. But what if a crowd gathers again? Starts that stupid chant. Ugh. No way. I'll pass.

At my old school, Jennifer and I played games like tetherball and handball all the time, but at some point, just before the summer, she seemed to lose interest and started spending more and more time with Trina Carlson and her groupies. I've never liked Trina. Seems like she's been popular since the third grade, and I swear, she's always had that "who farted?" look on her face.

"And she's so bossy. Thinks she's queen of the universe," I said once. But Jennifer shook her head.

"That's not true at all," she said. "Besides, what's so bad about being popular?"

"Well, *that's* not the problem. It's *her.*"

"She's super cool, Stevie," Jennifer insisted.

So one day, I ditched tetherball and went to join Jennifer. She, Trina, and some other girls were talking about who liked who and what boys were cutest. Really boring stuff, if you ask me. Still, I tried to be a part of the conversation.

"I think Paul likes Nicole," I said. "She told me he's started taking her route home lately and even asked her if she wanted to get a soda with him." Then I added, "She said he gets super shy. Turns red as a tomato and everything." I thought that last part was kinda funny so I let out a little laugh, but I quickly realized I'd said something wrong. The other girls all shot frowns my way and Trina's lips got all tight.

"Nobody asked you, Stevie," she snapped.

I turned to Jennifer, my eyes begging to know *What'd I say?* But she just huffed a disappointed sigh and turned her back to me. The next day, during quiet reading time, I finally figured it out when I saw Trina drop a note in Paul's lap on her way to sharpen her pencil. From the sharpener, she turned and looked at him with puppy-dog eyes and a big goofy smile. Sheesh. I wish someone had just *told* me she liked him.

"Stevie!" The tetherball game has come to an end, but it takes me a second to realize that Ally is looking up at *me*. Calling *my* name.

"Hello?" She waves a hand in front of me like she's trying to break me from a trance. "Come on!" She motions me toward her. She wants me to play. I feel Kenny look over, too. Ugh, why can't he just mind his own business? I feel my chest tighten with nervousness, but I'm excited at the same time. I just wish they'd all stop looking at me.

Be brave, Stevie.

I climb down—but just as my feet hit the sand, the bell sounds.

Rrrrring.

Recess is over.

"You got lucky!" Ally says with a laugh, and calls behind her, "Saved by the bell!"

After school, Mom takes me to the library. I love the library. The feeling I get when I first walk through the doors is electric. It's completely silent, but with brains buzzing. So quiet you could hear a pin drop. Or, as Mona says, so quiet "you can hear a mouse piss on cotton"—which Mom says I am *not* allowed to repeat.

Most people are reading, while some browse the walls lined with every kind of book you could think of. It's cool and clean and smells chalky and sweet. I think the library is a kind of church.

"I'll be over there," I whisper to Mom, pointing at the kids' section.

She nods and says, "Okay."

Before long, I have stacks and stacks of books on the table next to my bag. I know I'm going to have to narrow them down. Ten is the library's limit and five is Mom's. She's afraid I might lose one. Even though I never have!

It takes me a while, but I'm finally satisfied that I've found my five. Two Judy Blume books: *Otherwise Known as Sheila the Great* and her brand-new one, *Blubber*. I also got three books on Hollywood and the movies. They're all filled with glossy black-and-white pictures of starlets in silky gowns. Of faraway eyes. There are lots of photos from films I've seen, too. The pictures take me back to the movies and make me feel like I'm watching them all over again.

I'm settled deep in one of the library's beanbag chairs, lost in my book, when my stomach lets out a growl as mean as a rabid bobcat. I look up to be sure no one else heard it. The library worker shelving books to my right quickly turns her eyes away from me, pretending to be intrigued by the cover of the book she's holding. My belly lets out another loud growl, and this time I pull all my books onto my lap, hoping to at least muffle the noise. I'm getting seriously hungry. Mom hasn't come over to nudge me into leaving yet. She always does. When Mom goes to the library (or the supermarket, or the mall) she always knows exactly what she's getting. Never strolls through browsing, stumbling upon unexpected choices. Nope. She barrels in like a heat-seeking missile, zeroes in on her target, and snatches it up. No lollygagging. She's quickly ready to go home. But today *I'm* the one ready to go first.

I gather up my books and travel across the library in search of her. I wander through all the adult sections, but I don't see her at any of the tables. I cross to the back wall and begin searching the aisles of books. It takes me a while, but finally I spot her way in the back, in a corner, talking to someone. A tall Black man in an African dashiki. Clear, frameless glasses rest low on his nose. His head is shiny and bald as a bowling ball.

The man sees me approaching, and a smile spreads over his face. But, instead of speaking to me, he says something to my mom, hands her a book, and walks away. Mom turns to me, smiles.

"Hey, pumpkin. You ready to go?"

"Who was that?" I ask.

"He works here," she says.

And sure enough, when we go to check out, the bald man walks behind the desk and takes our books.

"Oh, *Old Hollywood*," he says, admiring a book with movie stars Carole Lombard and Clark Gable on the cover.

"They're our favorites, right, Mom?" I tell him, looking up to my mom.

"Uh-huh," she says, and turns to the man. "I've always liked the old movies best. And the Friday Night Movie is our special movie night!" She gives me a squeeze.

When we get home, I lay the beautiful books out on my bed and gaze at the satiny images on their covers.

I examine my reflection in the dresser mirror. I lift the thick pile of hair from my ears and neck and try to imagine what it would look like rolled up on the sides like Lana Turner's. Holding my hair up in a high roll, I do my best to imitate the glamorous poses from my book covers, but this hair ain't gonna cut it. I run to Mom's room and snag the Ava wig from its foam head. Back in my room, after lots of tucking and adequate pinning, I pull the wig onto my head and smooth out the silky waves. I part my lips and drop my eyelids to half-mast like I'm tired. Like I'm bored. Like I'm a movie star.

"Ooh. Drama!" Naomi says, laughing, and pushes my cracked door open wide. She walks to my bed. "Hollywood glamour!" She plops down and begins flipping through one of the glossy books.

"Do you like old movies?" I ask her, but she just shrugs. "Mom and I love them."

"Some are okay. Not really my thing, though." She tosses the book back onto the bed, then turns and studies my reflection in the mirror. She lifts a curl of the wig from my shoulder and then lets it fall. "I like your natural hair better."

As she starts to leave I say, "The Friday Night Movie is on tonight. Watch with us. You might like it."

Naomi grins and nods. "Thanks, cuz. I might do that."

I spot the small button pinned to her jean jacket. An orange circle with a big black cat lurching forward.

"All power to the people," I read aloud.

"Oh!" Naomi quickly unpins the button and shoves it in her jeans pocket.

"That's cool looking," I say. "You should keep it on."

"Yeah, but...," she starts, then smiles and shakes her head. "Don't want it to get ruined, you know?"

After dinner, Mom announces, "I need to run out, pumpkin. I shouldn't be long."

But next thing you know it's eight o'clock and the Friday Night Movie is starting. Mom still isn't home.

Upstairs, Naomi's listening to music. Dad's out. He always works late Friday nights.

I go ahead and tune into the movie even though I've seen it before. Usually I wouldn't care. Not if Mom were here. If she were here, we'd talk about our favorite parts that were coming up, about new things we noticed. But watching it again all by myself? That isn't any fun.

I fall asleep before the movie ends, and when Mom finally does come home, I'm too tangled in my dreams to break free and wake enough to say something to her. I feel her cover me lightly in a blanket, and the room goes black as she cuts the light.

Chapter Eight

It's been a week since Mom said she got tied up at Mona's helping her with her television and missed our movie night.

"But tonight we're going to watch together *for sure*, right?" I say.

"You know, Stevie, I do have a few things I promised to do for Mona, but I'll try to get back in time. If I'm not, you should watch with Naomi. I'll bet she'd love that." Mom brushes a red coat of polish over the top of her pinkie nail.

"Are you kidding? She'll be gabbing all night with all her new friends!" I say. I can't believe Naomi has already made friends. Loads! In just *one* week! It's so unfair! "Did you tell you that she got invited to a sleepover tomorrow night?"

"Yes. It's good news for her, Stevie," Mom says.

"I know. I'm not saying it's bad or anything, I just, I don't know. Did you tell her she can?"

"I did," she says, sighing and doing her best to screw the top back on the nail polish without mussing her perfect new manicure. "Listen, pumpkin, you're going to find new friends in no time. Just be sure you let them *see* you. Those new friends can't find you if you're hiding yourself away. I know what you're like."

I shrug. Mom's always so optimistic, but this time, I think she's wrong. No one is interested in being friends with me. They've all got friends already. Letting them *see* me isn't going to make a difference.

The phone rings.

"I'll get it!" I run to the kitchen. "Hello?" I say into the receiver. At first there's no response. I'm not even sure there's still someone on the line. I listen but hear nothing. I ask again, "Hello?"

"Yes..." It's a man. His voice is deep and calm as the sea. "Hello," he continues. He's speaking so slowly.

"Hi?" I don't think he has the right number.

"Yes, how are you?" But this time he doesn't wait for me to answer. "Is Katherine at home?"

Katherine? It's weird to hear anyone call my mom that. Everybody calls her Kitty.

"Who's calling?" I ask, but before he has a chance to

answer, Mom has carefully lifted the phone from my hand, sure not to smudge her wet nails. She waves me toward the living room.

"Hello?" she says. "You did? Oh! Thank you. I really appreciate that."

"Who is that?" I ask her. But instead of answering, she walks to the balcony, cradling the phone in her shoulder. She slides the glass door closed behind her. I strain and strain but can't make out a word.

I sprint through the house to the phone in my parents' room and ever-so-quietly lift the receiver and cover the mouthpiece so my breathing can't be heard. I know this is serious snooping and Mom would be so mad if she knew I was doing this, but I wouldn't have if she'd just told me who was on the phone.

"Last week was a lot for me," says Mom, laughing a little. "I'm overwhelmed. But I'm loving it."

"I know what you mean," says the man. "Have you spoken to your husband yet?"

"No," she says. "I can't let him find out. If he does, he'll put an end to it for sure."

"I understand," he says. "See you later?"

"Yes. See you."

My brain is spinning. Who *was* that? Dad can't find out *what*?

I carefully hang up the phone and dart downstairs to the hall bathroom. I close the door behind me so gently Mom can't possibly hear. I flush the toilet, wash my hands, and exit as though I were in the bathroom the whole time. When I get back to the living room, Mom is off the phone and entering from the kitchen, blowing on her nails.

"Who was that man?" I ask casually, sitting in front of the TV and turning the channel knob.

"Huh?" She's frowning, trying to repair a nick to her manicure.

"On the phone?" She has to know who I mean.

"Oh. Just a friend," she says. She grabs a bottle of polish and still doesn't look at me.

I want to ask her *what* was "a lot" for her last week, and *where* she was last week—but of course I can't.

"I need the nail polish remover," she says under her breath as she stands and heads for the stairs. As she passes me, she laughs a little as she says, "So nosy." I know very well what that means.

Stop asking questions, Stevie!

But I can't just ignore this.

After dinner and a bath, Mom announces that she has to run out.

"But Mom, the movie! It's seven p.m., it's nearly time."

"I told you I have to do a few things first." She looks

frazzled but manages to give me a quick kiss on the top of my head anyway. "I should be back in time to catch it with you. If not, start without me."

Start without her? Again? Doesn't she know that half the fun is watching *together*?

Once Mom leaves, I head to her closet to play dress-up. I'm upstairs, decked out in long gloves and sequins, when I hear Dad come through the front door.

"Dad!"

I only meant to be upstairs for a minute, but when I get to the bottom of the stairs and see the TV, I realize I've missed half the movie already. I must've really lost track of time.

"Heya, kiddo! Where's your mom?" Just what I was wondering. Dad walks to the kitchen calling for her. "Kitty?"

"She said she had to do some errands and stuff," I say.

He comes back holding a pork chop. "Oh yeah? This late?"

"I dunno," I say. "She didn't make it back for the movie." I wonder if I should tell Dad about the man on the phone. But I'm pretty sure it will just make him mad, and I've definitely heard enough of my parents arguing to last a lifetime.

"What were you guys supposed to be watching?" Dad

asks. I point to the TV and he makes a face. "Oh, one of her old movies, huh?" He walks over and turns it off. "I have a better idea."

Seated at the kitchen table, Dad and I play poker and drink root beer. We've dumped the loose coin jar out and are using the pennies and nickels as chips.

"Okay, I'll take two new cards," Dad says as he sets his old cards off to the side. I deal him two fresh ones. I swap out three cards for three fresh ones and we both sit back and contemplate our hands.

"You're getting pretty good at this," he says. "I think I'd better watch out."

"Yeah, you'd better," I say.

"Oh, okay smarty. I'll bet two coins." He pushes two pennies into the center of the table.

I've got a pretty good hand so I'm not scared.

"I'll meet your two and raise you two more," I say, pushing more coins to the middle.

"Ooh," he says. "You're scaring me, kiddo....Okay, I fold!" He tosses his cards down. "Whatcha got?"

"Nope! I don't have to show you," I say, quickly mixing my cards and his with the deck cards.

"Ah, now! Who taught you that?" he gripes.

"You did!" We both crack up and I get to shuffling.

Two more games and I'm pretty pooped. I'm about

to get up and go to bed when Dad asks, "So, how're you spending your lunches at your new school?"

"What do you mean?" I ask. But I know what he means. He wants to know if I've made friends.

"I'm guessing you're finding a private corner somewhere and eating your baloney and cheese all by your lonesome."

"Well, it's not my fault," I say. "It's not like I don't *want* someone to eat with."

"I know, kiddo," he says. "I'm sure you do. But you're a cool kid. I just hope you don't hide yourself away from everyone."

"I don't."

"Well, good," he says. He pushes his chair back and stands. "I'm in need of a shower and then I'm taking these tired bones to bed!"

When Dad walks out of the kitchen, I take a look at the clock over the doorway and can't believe Mom still isn't home. But I'm in no mood to wait up for her.

I go to the kitchen cabinet and pull one large pot, one small one, and two medium-sized pans from the cupboard. I scoop a handful of silverware from a drawer and go to the living room.

Carefully, I stack the pots and pans on top of one another as precariously as I can just behind the front door.

I lay the silverware across the pot openings. When Mom comes in and opens the front door, the entire tower will crash down. It'll be loud enough to wake me so I can come down and tell her how mad I am that she missed the Friday Night Movie *again*.

Upstairs, Dad's in the shower, so I go straight to my room and climb in bed. I start thinking about that call again.

What could that man have been talking about? What doesn't Mom want Dad to know about? I don't even know who this friend is and she's sharing a secret with him. Something she won't even tell *me*. And what errands could keep her out of the house for so long? Even Dad thought that was weird.

I have no idea how long I've been sleeping when I awaken to the explosion of crashing metal followed by Mom's cursing.

"Damnit!"

She never curses.

Did I go too far? Maybe I shouldn't have done that after all. But *I'm* the one who should be mad. She *promised* she'd be back for the movie this week after missing last week.

I'm on my way downstairs to ask where she's been, to remind her she missed the movie, when I hear Dad storm out of the bedroom.

"Where've you been?" I hear him asking. Well, not asking. Demanding.

"Did you do this? What is wrong with you, Cooper?" I can hear her collecting the pots and pans, walking to the kitchen. He's following and still asking questions, and soon they're at it again. Arguing.

And this time it's definitely all my fault.

Chapter Nine

Does your mom have any Kotex?"

"Kotex?"

"You know, pads. For her period?"

"Oh, uh…" I don't know a lot about periods yet, but I do know they can make you grumpy, kind of like Naomi's acting now. She's been stomping through the house all morning.

I shrug. "I don't know."

I haven't seen my mom since the night before. I couldn't face her this morning after the booby trap I laid for her last night. After causing another big fight between her and Dad. So I took my sweet time getting up and only heard her go out about a half hour ago.

Naomi looks around the room like the answer to her

discomfort is painted on the walls in pale ink. She pounds on her stomach with a closed fist.

"Okay," she says, turning to me. "Your mom had to head out, so you've gotta come with me. Besides, look at you! It's a gorgeous Saturday and you're still in your pajamas! You don't know how good you have it. Back home, when it's nice like this, we're out *all day*! Throw your shoes on. We're going to the store."

I direct Naomi—silk scarf tied over her hair and sunglasses hiding dark circles—to cut through the park. It's a faster way to get to Ocean Park Boulevard, where the nearest drugstore is. It's a perfect Santa Monica day. Warm, but not hot. Bright blue sky. Cloudless. At eleven a.m., the park is already full. Picnic bench birthday parties are in full swing. A patchwork of blankets covers the grass. Groups of girls and kissy-face couples stretch out, basking in the sun, eating, reading, and laughing.

As we pass some boys playing basketball, all their loud talk suddenly goes quiet and I can feel the attention of the entire court shift in our direction...to Naomi. She may have been feeling crummy all morning, but she senses the shift in the wind, too, and now she seems to stand a little straighter.

One of the boys breaks away from the group and is quickly walking alongside Naomi, but she manages to keep her gaze dead front. Still, she doesn't pick up her pace or do anything to shake him. She just kinda strolls, twirling her gold necklace with her forefinger.

"I seen you move in across the street," the boy says, walking backward so he can face her. He looks kinda like the guy from her album cover. All bad boy, bashful smile. "You going to Samohi?"

Bingo! That's Naomi's school, all right! Santa Monica High, but everybody calls it Samohi. I open my mouth, about to tell him so, but when Naomi just smirks and doesn't answer, I figure I should keep my trap shut, too.

"It's all good. I get it. Don't talk to strangers, right?" He swats my shoulder as he laughs at his own joke, like I'm one of his pals or something. But when he looks back to Naomi, I see his eyes find her orange button with the lunging black cat that she has pinned back on her jacket. He's still smiling but more direct now.

"I'm Jimmy," he says, reaching into his back pocket. He unfolds a sheet of paper and hands it to her. "Now I'm not a stranger."

I lean in to get a look at the flyer. There's a drawing of the same black cat from Naomi's button.

ALL POWER TO THE PEOPLE

There's a lot of writing on the flyer, too, but Naomi quickly folds it before I can read any of it. Finally she looks at Jimmy.

"It'd be good to see you there, sis," he says. "What's your name?"

"Naomi," she says, and smiles, picking up her stride again. But this time he doesn't follow, he just smiles back.

"I'll see you later, Na-o-mi!" he calls.

Judging from the grin on her face and the new pep in her step, I'm pretty sure Naomi's forgotten all about her period.

"He seemed nice," I say, hoping she'll add a little more, but she only nods, her grin widening a bit. "What'd he hand you? That paper?"

"Oh, uh...I think it's just some stupid party or something," she says. "He's crazy if he thinks I'm going." She laughs a little and quickly ducks into the drugstore. Ending any more discussion on the subject.

As soon as we're done and step out onto the pavement, Naomi decides she's hungry.

"Mom made bacon and eggs," I tell her.

"That's all cold and nasty now," she says. I don't argue. "I just wanna get some chips." She turns and heads for Surf Liquor a couple of blocks away.

Carload after carload of families pass by on their way to the beach. Kids crammed in the backs of trucks or spilling out of station wagons, their heads leaning out like cocker spaniels.

"You wanna go to the beach?" I ask. "Maybe not today, but—"

"The beach? Uh, not really," she says, and squinches up her face.

"What? You don't wanna go to the beach? Seriously? It's the best. You gotta go," I say.

"I mean, I'm sure I'll go, just not now," she says with a shrug. "Maybe some other time."

"You ever been?" I ask.

"Yeah...once."

"Did you like it?"

"It was all right," she says. "My dad took me. Just the two of us."

She smiles at me when she says this and I know she's telling me more than "Yes, I've been to the beach." She's telling me that the memory is a special one.

"I want to go with you," I say.

"You just *love* the beach, don't you?" she says, and laughs.

"I do!" I say. "We're going soon. It'll be really fun, Naomi! I promise!"

"Okay, okay," she says. "Maybe next weekend if it's hot enough."

We're about to cross the street for Surf Liquor when Naomi stops and points.

"Ooh, look! A Pinto! I see them everywhere here. I never used to see them in Boston," she says. I follow her finger and see the car she's pointing to. It's a navy-blue Pinto just like ours parked on the street in front of the library. As we get closer, I get a better look at it. It isn't just *like* ours, it *is* ours. It's my mom.

I don't get it. Why didn't she take me with her? She knows the library is my favorite place. And what's she doing there, anyway?

I'm about to say something to Naomi when I spot Kenny and Donald inside Surf Liquor. I stop walking. Naomi turns to me.

"What?" She catches me looking at the boys. "You know them? Oh, wait. You *like* one of them, don't you?" She grins and pokes my arm.

"*No!* Not even!" I say, but I am not going inside. "I'll wait here."

"Ooh, someone has a cru-ush," she sings.

I fold my arms and walk to the nearby bus bench. "No," I repeat. "I'll just meet you here, okay?"

Naomi hesitates, then asks, "Stevie, those boys aren't mean to you, are they?"

"Huh?" I'm not sure how to answer this. I mean, they

haven't pushed me around like they do Marcus, or any-thing. They're just jerks. And they started that Charmin thing, but...I don't want any trouble. "No. They're just jerks."

She studies my face a bit before saying, "Okay...okay. Well, you want something?"

"Funyuns and a Bubble Up, please."

"All right. Stay here, okay?"

I nod, and just as I turn for the bench, I hear, "Please don't squeeze the Charmin!" Kenny and Donald are on their way out of the store and have spotted me.

"What's up Charmin head?" Kenny calls, and they both start laughing. I just suck my teeth and head for the bench.

"Who you think you're talking to?" It's Naomi. Both boys stop and turn. The "Who me?" dumb look plastered across both of their faces. "That's right, I'm talking to *you*!" She jabs the air with her forefinger. "If you're trying to address my cousin, I suggest you call her by her name, got it?"

They give her a half nod before quickly picking up their step. Neither one so much as glances my way.

Naomi watches them leave, and when it's clear they're gone, she calls to me, "I'll be right back, Stevie."

Oh man. I wonder how I'm going to have to pay for that on Monday. There's no way Kenny and Donald will let that slide. I wish she hadn't said anything. But as I watch their tiny figures disappear over the hill in the distance, I'm glad Naomi called them out. Put a little scare in them. That was definitely some big-sister vibe right there. I like it.

As I sit on the bench looking at my mom's car across the street, I can't get over the fact that she'd go to the library without me. Maybe she just wanted to let me sleep in. Or maybe she's mad at me for the pots and pans. I should go say something to her. I wait for a moment when there are no cars coming and quickly dart across the street. There's a window just past the front grass and I lean against it, searching the room for a glimpse of her, but all I see are a bunch of stumbling babies bumping into each other and tumbling around on the floor while their moms huddle off to the side. The librarian is sorting books on a metal rolling shelf. There are a few people at tables, noses buried in books and magazines. But I don't see my mom.

Suddenly, someone approaches the window and I duck. I must look like a crazy person with my face pressed up against the glass like this. I wonder if my dad ran around peeking into windows, ducking at the last minute just before being discovered by the enemy. I inch my head back up just as the person walks away from the window. It's that same man I saw when I visited the library last time.

The one who was talking to Mom. He doesn't notice me at all; instead he turns and heads toward the back bookshelves.

I scan the rest of the small space but don't see my mom. Maybe she isn't in the library after all...but then I look back to where the man was and see my mom disappear behind the bookshelves there. I jump up and try to see where they're going.

But she's gone.

"Stevie!"

Naomi's across the street near the bus bench, a hand on her hip. I motion to the window, but she just shakes her head and storms across the street.

"What're you doing? You scared the crap outta me! I told you to stay put!"

"My mom's inside. That's *her* car," I say. "I was trying to see where she went."

Naomi looks past me inside the window.

"Thanks for saying something to those bullies from my school. I can't stand them," I say. But her eyes have locked onto something. She leans forward for a better look, and I turn to the window again to see what she sees.

It's my mom again. She's deep down one of the aisles in a corner talking to the bald dude.

"Who's that?" Naomi asks, studying them.

"I don't know," I say. "He works there." I bolt past Naomi to the front doors. As I pass her, I anticipate the exasperated beginnings of some sort of protest.

Stevie, don't go in there!

Stevie, what are you doing?

Let's just go, Stevie!

But she doesn't say anything and instead just lets out a huff and follows me inside.

When I march up to the table, Mom is sitting with several books open in front of her, sharing a laugh with her new best bud.

"Hi," I say as I plant myself in front of her, hands on my hips, a familiar pose she strikes for *me* when she wants an explanation. The two of them look up to me, laughs trailing off but smiles remaining.

"Stevie!" She gathers and stacks her books neatly beside her. "Say hi to Clarence. You remember Clarence, don't you?" He flashes a smile that showcases a gap in the center of his teeth wide enough to fit a whole other tooth.

"Hello, Stevie."

It's the voice from the phone call.

"Hi, Aunt Kitty," says Naomi, who has just caught up; her tone is apologetic. I don't know why it should be, though. If anyone should be apologizing, it's Mom. What is she doing here? With this "Clarence"? "We were grabbing some stuff at the store and just passed by. We didn't mean to bug you. Stevie saw the car and—"

"You're not bugging me at all," she says, turning to Clarence. "Clarence, this is my niece, Naomi."

"Enchanted," he says, bowing like some fairy-tale prince and pointing his smooth skull at Naomi. "I'll leave you all." He and Mom share a smile before he glides across the floor, disappearing behind a tall bookshelf.

Weirdo.

"What are you doing here?" I insist.

"Keep your voice down," Mom says, and points to the chair in front of me. I don't feel like sitting, but it wasn't a suggestion. "Naomi, you want to grab yourself a couple books? Need anything?"

"Oh, no. Thanks. We're going." She taps me and motions for me to get up.

I give Mom a look. *Answer my question.*

"I had some work of my own to do, Stevie. But go ahead and pick a couple of books. I'll bring them home."

I shake my head. I still have books at home from our last visit. And if she thinks that just letting me get more books is going to make things okay, she's got another thing coming.

"No," I say, and turn to follow Naomi.

Mom sighs. "I'll be home soon, girls."

Work? What *work?* Since when does Mom work?

Once we're outside, Naomi shoves the bag of Funyuns in my hand.

"Hey, I still haven't seen you skate. You any good?" Naomi's slipping the tabs from our soda cans onto her fingers like rings. She's doing her best to make what Dad calls "small talk" with me. Trying to make me forget about that whole weird incident with my mom.

"I don't know," I say. "I'm okay, I guess." Through the library window, I see Clarence saunter back over to Mom's table. Again! He stands and they talk.

I wish I knew what they were saying.

Naomi waves a hand in front of my face. "Leave your mom be, Stevie. Why don't you show me some of your moves? Get your skates. We'll go to the park."

The crowd in the park has thinned out by the time we get home, grab my skates, and get back. The basketball court is completely empty.

"Hey, look! It's all clear!" I run across the court, plop down on a side bench, and squeeze into my skates. Skating actually will help take my mind off Mom. And I'm looking forward to showing Naomi what I can do. I still can't jump, but I've gotten really good at snaking backward.

But even though *she's* the one who wanted to come to the park, Naomi straggles behind me, her face searching the grass, the jungle gym. She's looking in all directions and I suddenly realize she was hoping that Jimmy guy would be here.

I skate around for a while anyway and even though she says, "Great!" and "How'd you learn that?" I can feel her attention on every other area of the park. Thinking maybe he'll reappear.

Chapter Ten

Back at home, I hit my clubhouse. School has had me too distracted to fix it up, but I can't really decorate until I've had a chance to clean all the dust and cobwebs anyway.

I leave my box of magazines and stuff upstairs and with Mom's broom swipe at cobwebs in a corner. Their sticky wisps wrap around the broom's bristles like cotton candy. I hear the telephone ring upstairs and Mom's shoes shuffling across the floor as she goes to answer. But just as the phone stops ringing, I hear a loud *click* sound from somewhere near me, under the house. That's weird.... The phone must've set it off. But what made it? I've never heard anything like that down here before.

It sounds like it came from the tunnel. I look in that

direction, and sure enough, deep in the tunnel, I see a tiny red light. As I get closer, I see that the light is coming from a gray box that I'm sure wasn't there before. It rests on the floor of the tunnel, but its wires travel up the tunnel wall to one of the phone boxes. To the one marked "5." That's *our* apartment. I scoot up into the tunnel until I reach the box and, upon further inspection, see that it's a tape recorder. Jennifer's dad had one like it and we used to sing into it, recording ourselves and playing it back later, always wondering why we didn't sound quite as good on the recording as we did in real life.

There's a little plastic window and I can see the wheels of a cassette tape going round and round. It's recording something right now. Upstairs, Mom lets out a sharp laugh, says something I can't make out, and then the recorder again makes a loud *click*. The tiny cassette wheels have stopped. The red light has gone dim.

That call was being recorded! But who would be recording our calls? The phone company? Our new apartment manager? That doesn't seem right. For one thing, she hardly even knows us, and for another, she could get in big trouble for doing something like that. For invading our privacy. And why would she want to do something like that, anyway?

After a moment, it hits me. Who is the one person who would actually know anything about a recording device? The one person who would have no problem snooping around. Who would *spy* on other people.

Once a spy, always a spy.

This is my dad's handiwork.

But bugging the *house phone*? Why? What is he listening for? Is there some sort of danger we should all be worrying about?

I should tell Mom.

But wait. Maybe she was just talking to that Clarence guy again. Maybe the secret that Dad's not supposed to know about is on there.

I hover my finger over the rewind button. Now *I'm* doing some serious snooping. But how else am I going to find out what's going on?

I press the button and the tape squeals in reverse at super speed...and then it stops. I press play.

There's only a brief crackle and pause before Mom answers, "Hello?" But the voice on the other end isn't a male voice. It isn't Clarence. It's Mona. She needs Mom to pick something up for her at the pharmacy. When they hang up, I hit the stop button and hop down from the tunnel. I take the stairs up to the balcony two at a time.

I don't have to tell Mom I played the tape. I can just tell her that the recorder is down there. That Dad is recording us. But when I get to the kitchen, there's no sign of her.

"Mom!" I call.

"She went out!" Naomi shouts from the living room.

Right. The pharmacy for Mona. I guess I'll have to wait until she comes home to tell her.

I'm hungry, and with Mom's constantly ducking out, it's starting to feel like every man for himself as far as food's concerned. I peel back the tops of aluminum-foil-covered leftovers in the fridge, but nothing looks worth taking a chance on. I'll just have some strawberry milk. I go to grab a clean glass from the drying rack, and there, next to the rack, is a small pad of paper and a pencil. The phone is just off to the side.

When I first found out that my dad used to be a spy, I checked out loads of books on spy stuff: *How to Pick a Lock*, *How to Create Your Own Secret Code*, *How to Lift a Fingerprint*, and more. A lot of the stuff was too hard for me to understand at the time, but there was one trick of the trade I remembered well.

I take the pencil and very lightly run it across the top of the notepad—back and forth, back and forth—until I've covered most of the top piece of paper with a thin layer of pencil lead, then hold it up to the light. I can barely make out what my mom's written on the last sheet of paper, but it's there:

$$555\text{-}2305$$

A phone number. She must've written it down recently. It wouldn't be Mona's number. She knows that one by heart.

I write the number out more clearly: 775-2305.

I stare at it awhile before I finally decide to call. What's the worst that could happen?

I grab hold of the phone and dial the mysterious number. I don't have to say anything. I can just hang up. Jennifer and I used to prank call people all the time when we were little.

"*Hello?*" they'd answer.

Jennifer would lower her voice so she sounded just like a man.

"*Well hello,*" she'd say. "*I'm calling from GE Home Appliances. Is your refrigerator running?*"

"*Uh, yes, it is,*" they'd say.

"*Then you'd better go catch it!*"

No one ever knew who called. We just hung up.

The phone is ringing now. Just after the third ring,

there's the click of someone answering. They lift the phone and there's rustling and a breathy exhale before I finally hear, "Yes? May I help you?"

It's one of the deepest voices I've ever heard. Sounds like the guy from *Soul Train*. Like he's about to wish me "Love, Peace, and SOUL!"

But his voice also sounds familiar. My stomach tightens.

"Hello?" he says again. I cover the mouthpiece. "Hello? I can hear you there. Did you call the right number? Hello?"

I slam the phone down. It's him all right. That same guy who called here weeks ago. Library guy.

Clarence.

And suddenly I think I know why my dad is bugging our calls.

As soon as Mom comes through the door, I ask, "Where'd you take off to today? *Again?*"

She hands me one of the grocery bags and together we walk to the kitchen.

"I had to go to the store for Mona." Then she motions to the bags of groceries as we deposit them on the counter. "And I went to Lucky's."

"But...that's all?"

"Are you being nosy again, little lady?" She doesn't even turn around. "I don't think I was gone that long."

While her back is turned to me, I eye her open purse on the dining room chair. But I don't even know what I'm looking for.

"And Stevie, I really am sorry I wasn't back in time to see the movie last night, but...getting me back by setting up those pots and pans?" She laughs. "Okay, maybe I deserved it. But no more of that, got me?"

I nod.

"And what *was* that little scene at the library?" She turns to me. "I mean, I understand that you wanted to go, but sometimes I need to do things that don't necessarily concern you. And you need to respect that." She grabs a couple rolls of toilet tissue and exits through the hall.

Hmph. Maybe I shouldn't tell her about Dad's bugging the phone after all. She'll just say to mind my own business, that I'm being "nosy." And, most important, she'll get really mad at Dad, and they'll fight. Come to think of it, when she talks to that Clarence guy again, I'll finally hear the secret she's hiding. But I'll need to erase the tape right after. I can't take a chance on Dad's hearing her talking to that guy. Finding out she's been keeping a secret. He'll be so mad they might not just fight.

They might get divorced.

Chapter Eleven

As soon as I come through the classroom door Monday morning, I feel a strange swirl of excitement all around. Kids are pushing past me, racing to their cubby boxes. Everyone's beaming and laughing and it takes me a couple of minutes before I finally see what all the commotion is about.

Pomegranates.

There's one in every person's cubby. Mine included. A perfect little red ball of fruit with a pucker on top like the tie of a balloon. But with all the arms reaching, hands snatching, and elbows jabbing, I'm afraid I might sustain some serious injuries just trying to grab that piece of fruit. I wait for the crowd to clear before finally reaching into my cubby and taking hold of *my* pomegranate. It's really cool looking, but I'm not exactly sure what to do with it.

"Class! Take your seats!" Mrs. Quakely bellows from the front of the room. "For those of you who've just arrived on the planet, there are special treats in each of your cubbies. Mr. Quakely did a little harvesting this weekend and he insisted on giving each of you a small token of his appreciation. I may or may not have told him that you are my favorite class of the whole year."

"We're your *only* class of the year!" says Ally.

"Oh!" Mrs. Quakely pretends to be surprised by this news. "Well, maybe *that* explains it!"

The laughing and chattering rises in volume.

"Hey, hey!" She claps loudly. "Get your fruit and plant your bottoms. We have school to do!"

At recess, I'm sitting on a bench near the handball courts, unsure of how to open my pomegranate. As I look around, it seems everyone else has already figured that part out. Their fruit is all broken open, three or four pieces in their hands. Jewel-like seeds spill out across tables, and I see sticky, stained fingers everywhere.

Ally sees me sitting on the bench staring at my perfectly intact piece of fruit and stops.

"Best way to open it?" she says. "Smash it!"

I shake my head, confused. "What? I don't understand."

"On the ground. Do it!"

I look at the perfect fruit in my hand and consider

what she's saying. Smash it on the *ground*? *That's* what'll open it? I stand, hesitate, and look to Ally once more. Already, her entire mouth and even her cheeks are blushed a deep cherry from the sweet seeds. She nods vigorously. Okay. Here I go. I raise my pomegranate high and then dash it down onto the blacktop. It immediately shatters into four large chunks and I quickly scramble to scoop them all up.

"There!" Ally looks satisfied. And I think I am as well. "The seeds are so good. Chew them to get the juice." She takes a fat bite of her pomegranate, loading her mouth full of seeds. She chews and chews, grinning and making *yum* sounds, before she proceeds to *SPIT* the chewed seeds from her mouth one by one.

Yuck. I hate spitting. It's gross. And I guess my face says that I don't like it much, because Ally laughs.

"Aw! It's not that bad. Do it!" she insists.

I dig my teeth in and the sweet-and-sour juiciness lights up my mouth.

"Mmm!"

"Good, right?" she says.

I chew and chew and then, as funny as it feels at first to do it, I spit a seed out.

"There you go!" she says. I can't help but laugh. Mom would kill me if she saw me spitting.

Bing, bing, bing

I spit out three more. This is fun.

But just then, Ally spots trouble walking over.

"Oh boy," she says. "Here come your best buds. Looks like they have a present for you."

Kenny and Donald are sauntering over, pink-stained chins up and aimed my way. Kenny's got a chunk of pomegranate in one hand and the back of Marcus's shirt collar in the other. He's holding him up high and causing Marcus to walk on his tiptoes and for his arms to dangle awkwardly at his sides. Judging from his pained expression, Marcus is not up for this torture today. He doesn't nervously laugh or even fake a grin.

"What do you want, Kenny?" Ally starts, but just then, from back at our classroom door, Mrs. Quakely calls, "Ally!" and gestures for her to come. Ally waves back, and as she bounds off turns to Kenny again. "Why don't you just beat it?"

Kenny waves a dismissive hand after Ally. "Whatever," he says, and turns back to me. "Marcus wants to go steady with you," he says, shoving Marcus in my direction. Marcus stumbles and barely manages to keep from falling down completely. Donald lets out a loud cackle.

"You should totally take him up on it. Then *he* can fight your battles and you won't have to sic your cousin on people." He stares at me as he takes a large bite of his pomegranate.

"I didn't 'sic' her on anybody—" I start.

"Better yet, why don't you fight your *own* battles!" He spits a loogie of pomegranate seeds on the ground and gives me his best tough-guy face before walking off, Donald the weasel picking up the rear.

Marcus is tucking his shirt back in and straightening himself up.

"You okay?" I ask.

"Oh, me? I'm fine," he says, finally smiling. "Those guys just want to have their fun. They're not so bad really."

I shake my head and suck my teeth. "They're total jerks. You shouldn't let them push you around."

The bell sounds, and as I jog off to class, I hear Marcus say more to himself than to me, "You're probably right."

When I get home after school, Mom's car is gone. Inside it's quiet.

"Hello?" I call upstairs in case maybe Naomi's up there and on the phone. But no one answers. I toss my book bag on the couch and run out back and down to my future clubhouse.

I hop up to the recorder and press play, but the button just pops back up. I study the tiny tape through the plastic screen. It's rewound to the end. I guess there's no new call recorded. And I guess that's a good thing. Still, I'll have to keep my ears and eyes open. I can't give my parents any more reasons to fight.

Chapter Twelve

Even with her ginormous sunglasses, Naomi squints like an asteroid is aiming for her face. It's hard to believe she's ever been to the beach before. *Everything* is "icky" and "gross." Sand, seaweed. She does funny dances and arm shakes with every little bug she thinks she sees.

"C'mon, Naomi!" I call to her from the edge of the water. "The water's so nice!"

"I will! I will!" she shouts. But I'm not so sure. She's got her hair wrapped tightly in her silk scarf, every inch of it covered. On top of the scarf, she wears a super-wide-brimmed hat. Naomi gets her hair hot ironed every week. Either Mom does it or her friend Sandra does, and then she has to spend the rest of the week doing her best to keep it straight. I don't know how she manages. How are you supposed to stay out of the rain? How can you not go swimming in the ocean?

Once, after a day of styling Jennifer's bone-straight hair and playing in Mom's kink-free wigs, I asked Mom if she'd *please please please* press my hair for me.

"You sure? It's going to take a while to do. And then you have to take good care of it to keep it nice."

"Yes! I'm positively positive!" I said, turning to the mirror and flattening my puffy 'fro, already imagining my own head of silky locks.

The following Saturday, Mom pulled a chair into the kitchen near the oven and sat me down. She set a heavy iron comb directly on the stove flame and I watched it soak up all that heat while Mom greased my edges and braided my hair into sections, preparing to fry it into submission. The first time she brought the comb of fire near my face I tried my hardest not to move, but my body—my head really—just kept inching away from her.

"Stevie, you're going to have to sit still if you want me to do this."

I shut my eyes tight, didn't even breathe, as she brought the comb close. I felt the warmth of it near my temples and braced myself for contact, but it didn't scorch my skin. It didn't touch my skin at all. Instead, it sizzled its way through my oiled hair and I caught the smell of something toasting. My kinky curls. Soon to be completely flat. And, sure enough, two hours later, my whole afro lay limp. No longer reaching for the sky, my hair sloped toward the floor and obediently lay still over my shoulders.

"I'm not quite done," Mom said. "We have to give it a little shape." She reached for another iron instrument she'd set on the back burner of the stove, not a comb, but a large curling iron. She cooled it a moment on a hand towel before running it along a swatch of my hair and then wrapping the hair around it. The entire time she kept moving the chopstick handles so they made a *clack clack clack* sound. When she pulled the curler free, she offered the curl for me to hold.

"There," she said. I touched the twirled piece of hair and it felt like it belonged to the Ava wig, not to me. She curled my whole head that way and when she finally finished, she took a comb to it and fussed some more until she had it where she wanted.

I ran my hands over it while Mom went to get a hand mirror for me. It was smooth as could be and for the first time, I could feel my bony skull just underneath.

It rained the next day. Mom couldn't drive me to school so I pulled my raincoat over my head and kept my umbrella up the whole way to school, but by the end of the day, the rain had done its dirty deed and I was back to being a puff ball. Every attempt at straight hair has ended up the same; it gets rained on and is undone or I sweat too much and it frizzes up. Sometimes all it takes is a foggy day to unflatten it. My hair has fight. A little heat is not enough to keep it down.

So braids it is. I feel like a little kid wearing them, but after that first day, there's no way I'm wearing my hair out at school again.

Back at the beach, Naomi motions for me to go on into the water without her, then reaches into our beach bag and pulls out a foil-wrapped sandwich.

"Okay. But watch me," I say, and head into the water with my boogie board.

The sun is bearing down hard, but the ocean is cool and soothing. It feels so good. I'm always careful to go out just deep enough to be able to catch a wave, but not so deep that if a wave knocks me around I won't come up unable to feel the earth beneath my feet.

It's a while before the perfect wave finally lifts me and my board and sends us across the white, breaking water all the way to shore, delivering me to the sand like one of Poseidon's treasures.

When I stand, Naomi is at the water's edge cheering. But she's not alone. Jimmy from the park is standing next to her in swim trunks.

"Nice job!" he says.

"It took you all the way in!" says Naomi.

I run to her, trying to ignore her friend, and push the board into her hands.

"You try it!" I say.

"Oh no! I couldn't do that!" She laughs and hands it back to me.

"I'll show you," Jimmy insists.

Naomi ignores his offer and leads me back to the water. "Come on, Stevie, I wanna get my feet wet." She turns back to Jimmy and points to our bag of food. "Grab a sandwich."

I get Naomi to go in as far as her thighs, but then she starts screeching about the water's being too cold and she's ready to go back and lap up all of Jimmy's attention. Not only am I stuck having to watch them be all flirty and giggly with each other, but Jimmy's taken up my towel so I don't have anywhere to sit.

I head back into the water and stay in until my fingertips are raisins, only coming back after Naomi appears at the shore shouting.

"It's four!"

Mom said to meet her up at the boardwalk at four. Naomi gathers all our things and I quickly towel off. I look up and down the beach, but Jimmy is long gone.

We run as fast as we can across the burning-hot sand.

"Ow, ow, ow!"

Once we reach the boardwalk, we find a cool patch of grass and soothe our scorched soles. We slide our flip-flops on and get Bomb Pops from the ice cream truck while we wait for my mom.

"Here." Naomi hands me my Popsicle and a couple of napkins.

I lick the streaks of red and blue juice that stream down my hand and check both directions of the boardwalk for my mom. I search the streets beyond the beach, but I don't see her or her Pinto anywhere. It's 4:15, then 4:30, then 4:45.

"Don't worry, Stevie. I'm sure she just lost track of the time," says Naomi.

We sit under the shade of a huge palm tree and watch people navigate the tall balance beam and swing from the gymnast rings on the sand.

A bodybuilder, bulging flesh gleaming, has attracted a big crowd. He strikes poses for admirers. Takes photos. Signs autographs.

"That's too much muscle for me," Naomi says, and shudders.

It's a little after five when Naomi stands and points. "There she is."

Mom's Pinto is pulling up along the curb of a side street. She hurries to the walk, hand on her head to protect her wig from flying skyward like a summer kite.

"Mom!"

When she sees me, she waves and picks up speed.

"Sorry I'm late," she says, and motions for us to follow her.

"Where were you? It's so late." But she's paces ahead of me, navigating pedestrians and skateboarders. I'm not sure if she hears me.

On the ride home, I think about pushing my mom for an answer as to what kept her, but she and Naomi are talking and I feel like a nag so I let it rest.

Back at home, I use my key to let us in.

"Thank you, big girl," Mom says as she passes me and drags a hand across my damp head.

"I need a shower!" says Naomi on her way upstairs. "I feel so gross!"

The phone rings and I bolt for the kitchen to answer it.

"Your turn after she's done, you hear me?" Mom says. I hear her grumble something about trekking sand through the house as I pick up the receiver.

"Hello!" I sing.

"Hello yourself," a voice bellows on the other end. *That* voice. That guy. "Is Katherine there?"

"Hold on," I tell him. "Mom!" But she's already walking into the kitchen.

"Thanks, honey," she says as she takes the phone from me and smiles.

I've been checking the recorder for weeks and there's been nothing. I figured she was done talking to this guy. But he's calling...I'm finally going to hear what this secret is.

I start to head for my clubhouse when Mom stops me.

"Where do you think you're going?" she asks, holding a hand over the receiver.

"I—I was just gonna hang out in my clubhouse," I stammer.

"Nuh-uh. Not before a shower," she says. "Naomi will be out in a minute. Go on."

Dang! I need to get down there and listen to that call. To find out what's been going on. And then I have to erase it before Dad hears it.

Chapter Thirteen

When I'm done showering I climb into my pj's, and next thing I know, Mom's calling me down for dinner and it's too late for me to head down to my clubhouse without making her suspicious. Argh!

"Mona wants me to take her to church in the morning, but when I get back, how about we take a stroll along the mall?"

"That sounds great!" I say.

This is perfect. I'll wait until morning when Mom's out to play back the tape and then erase it before Dad can hear it.

When I get up the next morning, Mom is already gone and Dad's in the shower. Naomi is asleep... of course.

I quickly get changed out of my pajamas and hit the clubhouse.

I hop up and scoot, scoot, and scoot some more until I finally reach it. Looking through the little plastic window, I can see that some more of the tape has been used. Yes! I'm finally going to find out the truth. I hit rewind, and once it hits the end and the rewind button pops up, I turn the volume dial on the side of the recorder down a tad and press play. There's a crackle and then voices. But whose voices? It doesn't sound like Mom. I turn the volume dial up a bit. The man definitely isn't Clarence.

"I can't. We've got that march tomorrow," he says.

"Okay, then pick me up on your way. I wanna go," the woman's voice says.

"But you said you couldn't, 'cause—"

"Never mind that, stupid! I wanna go," she says.

"Stupid? What does that make you?" the man teases.

Oh. It's Naomi and Jimmy. Ugh.

I hit the fast-forward button, then play. This time, there's a long, silent pause before I hear my own muffled voice as I covered the receiver and called, "Mom!"

Once Mom is on the phone with Clarence and they finish their "Hi, how are yous," he says, "I got your message and that's not a problem at all."

"Meet you at the library?" she asks.

"Perfect."

They hang up and I'm left with nothing. No idea at all

what secret she's keeping from Dad. Just that she's meeting that guy. But somehow I think that's enough for Dad to get mad about. Enough for them to fight about.

The thud of my dad's footsteps across the living room above stops me cold. Is he moving to the front door? Or the stairs? He stops and then he starts for...the kitchen. He's definitely moving to the kitchen, and then he might go outside, and out to the balcony, then down here! I press rewind and let it go all the way to the top of the tape. Might as well keep Naomi's secret safe, too. When the button pops up, I set the recorder back where I found it, deep in the tunnel. I jump up, do my best to bang all the dust from my jeans, turn the flashlight out, and exit my clubhouse.

Dad isn't outside or up on the balcony, but I'd better not push my luck. I head inside.

He's pouring himself a cup of coffee in the kitchen.

"Heya, kiddo. Whatcha up to?" He licks powdered sugar from his fingers. "Mmm! These are good! Go ahead and grab yourself one. Might not be any left soon." He laughs and takes another doughnut with him as he heads out.

From the living room, Dad calls, "Stevie!"

I grab a chocolate glazed and go to him.

"Huh?"

"When your mom gets back from Mona's, tell her I went to meet Owen. Auction in Oxnard. Probably won't make it home for dinner. Can you do that, kiddo?"

"Sure."

Naomi had plans and couldn't join Mom and me for ice cream at the mall today. I had to bite my tongue to keep myself from shouting "Hallelujah!" Seriously! I can't tell you how good it feels to have Mom all to myself.

"Can I make a wish?"

The tiled fountain floor is covered in pennies. There are a few nickels and I count two dimes, but a penny is all you need for a wish.

Mom hands me her pistachio cone, and from her pretty gold coin purse she retrieves two pennies.

"You can make two," she says, taking back her cone.

I stand at the edge of the fountain, close my eyes, and focus hard on my first wish. I toss in my penny and smile at Mom.

"One more," she says. "But don't go wishing for the same thing twice."

How'd she know I was going to do that? But I guess she's right. A wish is a wish. Wishing it twice doesn't make it more powerful.

I wish my parents could be happy.

And I toss my coin in with the hundreds of other wishes. When I spin around to face Mom, I bump straight into a little girl on her way to make a wish at the fountain.

"Stevie!" she says, beaming. It's Lizzie. Jennifer's little sister. Before I can say anything, she's taken off in the other direction. "Jenny, it's Stevie!" Lizzie joins Jennifer and their mom and pulls on Jennifer's arm.

"Quit!" Jennifer snaps. Lizzie lets go and bolts back to the fountain.

"Hey!" I say, and wave. Mom swings around.

"Hi, Jennifer," says Mom.

"Hi."

Mom beams as she goes to Jennifer's mom, Elaine. The two of them quickly begin catching up on all that's happened in the months since our move. Jennifer slowly makes her way over to me at the fountain.

"Hi," she says, then looks at the glistening pool of copper. "Making wishes?" She smirks and I shrug.

"Yeah. I made a couple," I say with a laugh, and look at the coin-covered bottom. "I wonder how many of those pennies are *ours*!"

Jennifer just scoffs. "Lizzie was on her way over here to 'make wishes,' too." I catch the sarcasm in her tone. I never thought making wishes was a little-kid thing before, but sounds like that's what she's thinking. I quickly change the subject.

"Hey, so, I've been trying to reach you." I expect her to tell me how busy she's been with school this year, or how she's had to spend so much of her time watching her little sister. I expect she'll say something to let me know why she hasn't called me back, but she doesn't say anything, just kind of glances around the mall. Is she looking for someone? "Um, did you get Mr. Hutchinson? I know how much you hoped you would."

Jennifer nods and offers a half smile. Raises her eyebrows and blinks. "Yeah. He's cool." Then she cranes around to find her mom and I can tell she's ready to get moving.

"Hey, maybe we can do something for my birthday. It's coming up," I say to the back of her head.

"Mom!" She waves her mother to her, then turns back to me. "Yeah, maybe."

"Cool! I'll call you and we'll plan it out," I say.

"Uh-huh." Jennifer nods but seems to be in a hurry to go somewhere. She turns back to her mom. "Mom? We should go."

After they've gone, I tell Mom that Jennifer and I are going to do something special for my birthday.

"I think cake and ice cream is always nice," she says.

"Well, yeah, but I mean something else, too!"

"Like what?"

"Oh, I don't know. Jennifer and I will think of something good."

After we browse a few stores, Mom says there's no time for a movie.

"We'd better get back to the car."

Rounding the corner past Woolworth's, a young man wearing a black beret (like the French people wear) atop his tight afro steps up to Mom and hands her a leaflet.

"It'd be good to see you there, sister," he says, nodding and smiling.

Mom looks a little flustered but manages an awkward smile and a polite nod back. The man sees my eyes go to the button on his jacket, the same one Naomi has.

ALL POWER
TO THE
PEOPLE

When Mom turns away and begins reading the flyer, he reaches into his pocket and pulls out an identical button and places it in my hand.

"You too, baby girl."

He joins three other young men as they offer flyers and

talk to a Black teenage girl and a young white couple in ponchos and daisy crowns.

I look at my button, studying the big cat with its bared teeth.

Mom's shaking her head and crumpling the paper into a tight ball. She tosses it into the first garbage can we pass.

"What was that?" I ask. "Why'd you throw it out?"

"Those Black Panthers are troublemakers," she says, glancing at her watch. "Oh, Stevie, we'd better pick up speed. I need to get home. I let the time get away from me."

Taking two steps for her every one, I shove my new button deep in the pocket of my jeans.

As soon as we get home Mom announces that she has to run out and that Naomi's taking me to a movie.

I know right away what that means. Date night with Jimmy. Naomi insists on keeping him a secret. Making up lie after lie to cover for herself.

"I'm going to Sandra's to braid her hair."

"Sandra and I are going to check out the new Fox Hills mall."

"Tami, Sandra, and I are going to practice driving at the beach parking lot."

I finally asked Naomi why she didn't want to tell Mom about Jimmy.

"I don't need everyone all up in my business. Besides, if your mom finds out, she'll flip out, and then she'd tell *my*

128

mom, who would definitely have a full-blown hissy fit," she said, standing in front of the bathroom mirror, picking out and patting into place her fresh afro. Sandra trimmed and styled Naomi's hair so she can wear it natural, and ever since, I swear she spends even *more* time in front of the mirror than she did before! "Jimmy's older than me—he just graduated. And he's into some work that they just wouldn't be down with. They'd freak. No way." She spritzed a cloud of oil all around her hair, gave it a few more careful pats, and then smiled at her reflection before crossing to the hall. At her bedroom door, she whispered, "It's our secret, okay?" then turned a pretend key at the corner of her mouth.

I did the same. So, while I still don't really get what the big deal is, I keep my mouth shut, even when we go to the movies. And when we do, *I* have to lie a little and say that we took the bus. Not that we walked to the corner, where Jimmy picked us up and drove us to the theater in his Chevy Camaro.

"We're going to see *Cleopatra Jones*," Naomi says. "I can hardly wait for you to see this movie, Stevie. This sista blows all those lily-white movie stars your mom loves out of the water. She's Black, beautiful, *and* can kick ass. But it ain't a kid movie, so tell your mom we saw *American Graffiti*."

As we pull up to the theater, I get a look at the poster for the movie in the window. Wearing a short fur jacket with an automatic weapon on her arm, Cleopatra Jones looks like she means business. Yeah. I can see that this definitely isn't a kid movie.

6′ 2″ of Dynamite
and the
Hottest Super Agent Ever!

Jimmy looks at the poster and shakes his head. "She's hella fine!" Then he turns to Naomi and says, "But don't be jealous, girl. You finer than her any day of the week!"

We're early, so we have to wait in the parking lot of the movie theater. Naomi and Jimmy are sitting in the front seat with me in the back.

Naomi swats at Jimmy and laughs. "Yeah, right!"

"I'm telling the truth," he says, then pulls her to him. "Come here, beautiful." They lock faces *again*. Ugh. It's definitely *the* worst part of having to tag along with Naomi.

I turn and look out the window to the theater. "I think it's time we go inside," I say. "I wanna get some popcorn before the movie starts."

They break and Jimmy says, "Stevie girl, reach in my jacket back there and pass me my Kools. We'll go in after I have a smoke."

I rummage through the pockets of his leather jacket and find the soft green-and-white pack of cigarettes. When I pull them out, a folded piece of paper falls into my lap. Naomi snatches the pack from my hand and shakes two free. She pushes the dashboard lighter in, pops both cigarettes between her lips, lights them, then places one in Jimmy's mouth. Naomi deeply inhales, then tilts her head back and clicks her jaw on the exhale, again and again, making smoke rings. Jimmy sticks a finger through the last ring and grins at Naomi. She quickly turns her head to the back seat and meets my eyes as she tosses me the pack. I read her *do not tell!* loud and clear.

After she turns to face forward, I slip a single cigarette into the fold of my knit beanie before stashing the pack back in Jimmy's pocket. I'm about to put the folded paper back, too, but first I unfold it and see that same black cat from the flyer he gave Naomi when they first met. The cat from Naomi's orange button. From *my* button.

BLACK PANTHER PARTY
BLACK POWER AND ITS CHALLENGES
A DISCUSSION

There's more about food and music, but I don't want to get caught reading Jimmy's stuff so I shove it back in his pocket before I can see all of it.

The Black Panthers must be some kind of club. And according to Mom, they're a club of troublemakers. But that name sure is cool. And the picture of the black cat. *I* need a cool picture for *my* club. It'd help if I at least had a *name*.

Once in the theater, Naomi directs me to a seat and sticks a bucket of popcorn in my lap.

"We'll just be right over there if you need us," she says, pointing to the back of the theater.

The seats on either side of me are empty and I quietly hope they'll stay that way, but as the theater begins to quickly fill up, a mother and her two teenage boys start edging down the aisle toward me. They grumble between each other about who has to sit next to me until finally the mom, sweaty and wide-bodied, sighs heavily and squeezes her rear end into the tight seat. She huffs and puffs as she disburses refreshments. After a moment, she turns and gives me the once-over.

"You all alone?" she asks, eyebrows raised in concern.

"My cousin's back there," I say, and aim my finger in the direction Naomi disappeared to. The lady turns her head a little that way but doesn't really look. Instead, she nods at me, satisfied that someone's watching out for me. I'm not interested in sitting next to Naomi and Jimmy while they make out anyway. I'm just hoping that I don't get scared. I've never seen a movie like this before.

Finally the lights dim and the rumble of chatter softens. I look down at my bucket and realize I've almost finished my popcorn already.

Turns out the movie isn't scary at all. I've seen scarier at home on the couch. Mostly it's a lot of shooting and action stuff. But not a lot of blood, and the only blood I *do* see looks like red paint.

It's actually pretty awesome!

The best part of the movie is definitely the hero. Cleopatra Jones is the coolest person I've ever seen!

She could beat up all the evil girls and guys in the movie. Tall, brown, and beautiful.

And she has a big afro! Like mine!

Cleopatra Jones stalks through an abandoned warehouse like a lion in search of a zebra dinner. She leans against a metal door and then suddenly, with all her might, turns and kicks it open to reveal a blazing Southern California afternoon. I have to shield my eyes from the screen it's so bright. I take the opportunity to try to locate Naomi and Jimmy. They're not hard to spot. Six rows back, faces locked in a deep, tongue-entwined kiss. So much for discussing the movie after. They probably haven't seen *any* of it!

After the movie, Jimmy takes us home, but my mom still isn't back.

"Come in for a few minutes," Naomi tells him as she exits the car. Jimmy hesitates, then looks at me in the back seat. I have no idea what to say. Seems risky to me. Naomi turns back to us, still in the car.

"You fools better hurry before Aunt Kitty gets back."

Jimmy's totally silent and practically walking on tiptoes. I can tell he's really nervous about being in the apartment.

"Now, Stevie, I don't think I need to tell you this, but—" Naomi starts.

"I know, I know. Top secret," I say, and turn the pretend key at the corner of my mouth.

"That's my cuz!" She laughs.

In no time, Naomi's whipped up a bowl of mini ravioli and a glass of strawberry Quik. She deposits them in front of me, then gives Jimmy a shove toward the hall, both of them laughing at some inside joke as they head upstairs to continue their make-out fest. Ech!

Outside, there's a party at a neighbor's house somewhere. Laughter and music spill out onto a balcony. I finish my food, then go to the sliding glass door that leads to the backyard and step out. Night-blooming jasmine kisses the air. I breathe in its honeyed aroma, trying to hold it in my lungs. Upstairs, Naomi cranks up the volume on her record player so loud that now I can't tell where that party is.

I pull off my beanie to scratch my head and a thin white cigarette falls free. I'd forgotten about it!

I run back inside and rummage through the drawers of the kitchen. I find rubber bands, pens, broken pencils, Scotch tape. Where are the matches? Finally I spot a worn pack from one of the restaurants my folks like to go to. There are only two flimsy matchsticks left. I grab them and head out back.

I prop the door to my clubhouse open with a rock. Turn on the flashlight. It's way too scary to be in here with the door closed at night.

The cigarette is bent a little, but it doesn't look like it has any breaks in it. I put the spongy end in my mouth and strike the match.

I hold the flame to the end of the cigarette and pull on it the way I've seen Naomi do. The rush of smoke comes fast—and chokes me good. I'm coughing like that square kid in all the movies. I can't seem to stop. Fortunately, no one can hear me with the music upstairs blasting.

Once I stop coughing and catch my breath, I try again. A small puff this time. I balance the cigarette between my forefinger and my middle finger, tilt my chin back, and blow it into the dark, clean sky. With a hand on my hip, I'm Bette Davis. Or, wait...I wonder if Cleopatra Jones smokes.

I can't wait to tell Jennifer. I'll bet Trina Carlson has never smoked a cigarette.

After only two more hits, I start to feel queasy. I don't like the feeling at all. A little like the time we took a ferry to Catalina Island. I was nauseous for a whole week. I hope this isn't like that. I really hope this goes away quickly. I drop the stub on the ground and stomp it out.

Before I return the flashlight and head back upstairs, I flash it at the small tunnel and see that Dad's recorder is still there.

I hop up into the small space, scoot to the box, and push the eject button. The cover to the cassette tape pops open. I pull the tape free, but it looks brand-new. Like it hasn't been used yet.

Something crawls across my neck, and as I swat at it I feel the quick pinch of what is no doubt a splinter in my arm.

Or did something bite me?

Suddenly I feel like I'm covered in spiderwebs. Possibly covered in *spiders*! I shove the cassette back into the player and hurry out of the tunnel as fast as I can, batting away at my neck and head. I jump down and run outside, shaking out my shirt, dusting off my head, and trying to knock away the spiders and webs I'm sure I've collected.

Once I'm sure I'm spider-free, I stop and listen. I can hear the nearby party again. Naomi must've turned the music down. And then, the sound of the party is drowned out by the sound of a car pulling up in front of our building. As the engine runs, I hear voices. I go to the side gate, peer over it, and, stepping out of a long, turquoise-colored Cadillac with a white top is my mom.

I hear a low male voice growl something to her as she closes the car door and then leans on the window frame. Her body blocks my view of the driver, but there's no time to try to figure out who it is now. I have to warn Naomi and Jimmy.

I run inside and take the stairs two at a time. Bang loud and fast on her bedroom door.

"What?" she screams in her most irritated tone before pulling the door open hard. "What do you—"

"Mom's here! Walking up right now!" I say.

Jimmy darts past me fast but freezes just before running down the stairs when we hear the front door open.

"I'm home!" Mom calls.

We *all* freeze. Naomi's hand goes to her mouth and her eyes fill with terror. Jimmy raises his hands up to his sides as if to say, "What do I do?"

I take a moment, looking back and forth between the two of their perplexed faces, before bolting past Jimmy and down the stairs.

"Hi, Mom!" I run to her and throw my arms around her.

"Hey, pumpkin," she says, and kisses the top of my head. "How was the movie?"

"It was good," I tell her. I pull my arms from around her waist and grab hold of her hand, leading her toward the kitchen. I make sure to speak a little more loudly than usual. "But I'm starving! Could you *please* make me something to eat?"

"Didn't Naomi feed you?" she asks, tossing her purse onto the couch.

"Yeah, but I'm hungry again," I whine as I drag her down the hall.

"Okay, okay," she laughs. "I'm pretty hungry myself."

While Mom pulls food from the fridge and cabinets, my heart is racing. Her mouth moves, but I don't hear a single word she speaks. Instead, I listen to the tiptoes of careful feet on the stairs and the slow and steady drag of the living room glass door sliding open and then closed.

"Do you know what I mean?" she asks. I nod and smile and, thankfully, it's enough. She places a peanut butter and jelly sandwich and a glass of milk in front of me and smiles.

"Hey, Aunt Kitty!" Naomi says as she enters the kitchen. She lays a hand on my shoulder. "Girl, you sure have an appetite."

"Hi, Naomi." Mom takes another plate from the cupboard. "You want one, too?"

"Thank you, yes." When Mom isn't looking, Naomi mouths the words, "Thanks, cuz!"

I nod and give her a thumbs-up.

It feels kinda good to be her partner in crime.

Chapter Fourteen

On Monday when I come home from school I hear raised voices in the kitchen. But not the usual Mom and Dad. Instead, it's Mom and *Naomi*.

"I don't care. It's not mine!" Naomi storms down the hall and straight upstairs without so much as a "What're you looking at?" to me as I stand there in shock.

Mom and Naomi don't *ever* fight. I've never even heard them raise their voices to each other.

I drop my bag near the door and run to the kitchen. Mom is washing her hands and mumbling to herself.

"What happened?" I ask.

"Oh," Mom says, turning to me in the doorway. She cuts the faucet and dries her hands on the plaid dish towel. "Your dad found this downstairs, and...I just can't stand *lying*," she says. On the kitchen counter, sitting atop a small swatch of paper towel, is a tiny cigarette butt.

Mom kisses the top of my head and walks out. I hear her climbing the stairs and making her way to Naomi's room. I guess the fight's not over. Naomi's right. It's a good thing Mom doesn't know about Jimmy if this is how she reacts to a cigarette.

Just then, I realize something.

I run to my clubhouse. There, I grab the flashlight and shine it all along the floor, but it's gone. The cigarette butt. *My* cigarette butt. It's nowhere to be found.

Oh man. Naomi's in trouble because of *me*. I flash the light all around to be sure. And then at the tunnel—but I have to walk closer to be sure of what I see there. Or more like what I *don't* see.

The recorder is gone, too.

Dad must've thought that *whoever* was smoking down here was bound to spot the recorder and blow his cover. And he knows that if *Naomi* finds out, she'll be sure to shout from the mountaintops that her uncle is secretly recording the entire family. She already hates the CIA! Yeah, I'm pretty sure he removed it as a precaution. He doesn't suspect that I know.

Looking around the room, I think of Jennifer and how I need to get her over here to help decorate this place. When

I saw her at the mall, I forgot to tell her all about the cool clubhouse we can make. And we have to start planning my birthday celebration! We need to think of something cool to do. It's only a month away.

I use the kitchen phone to call Jennifer so Mom and Naomi can have plenty of space upstairs.

She picks up after the first ring.

"Hurry and get over here, Mel!" she says, laughing into the phone. Another girl is there with her, laughing and talking.

"Um, hey…" I force an awkward laugh. "It's…it's not Mel. It's Stevie." I definitely hear the rustle of something covering the mouthpiece.

Finally Jennifer says, "Oh, hi. What's up?"

"Well, my birthday is coming up and I was thinking we should get to planning, you know?" Another long pause while something covers the mouthpiece again. This time, when she moves her hand, I think I hear someone say "just hang up" in the background before Jennifer speaks.

"Oh yeah. I'll have to call you back," she says.

"Oh, that's cool. When were you—" I start. But before I can finish…

"Okay? Bye!"

She's gone.

Stupid Trina Carlson. I'd know that snotty voice

anywhere. Telling Jennifer to "hang up." What a jerk. And that "Mel" she was expecting on the phone is definitely Melinda. Hmph. *Mel.*

Whatever!

I know that Trina and Melinda don't wanna hang out with me, and I guess that makes it awkward for Jennifer. But I just wish she wasn't friends with them at all. Well, we'll just have to talk later when those jerks aren't around.

The next day after school, I'm headed for the north gate, where all the parents gather for pickup, when Ally runs up alongside me.

"You getting picked up today? Don't you just live by the park?" Ally's breath smells like strawberries, and I must be squinting at its sticky sweetness, because she reaches into her pocket and offers me a piece of Bubble Yum.

"Thanks," I say, nodding and unwrapping the pink cube. "My mom's taking me to the library."

"Cool," she says, and points to a mustached man waving wildly from the hood of a yellow station wagon. "That's my dad."

Leaning on the hood of every other car is a mother or two, there to pick up their kids. Ally's is the only father.

"Oh. Cool," I say. Then, "Your mom doesn't pick you up?"

"This is *his* week. My parents got divorced over the summer, so now I have *two* houses," she says with a laugh.

Divorced. Just like Kenny said.

I don't know if it's okay to laugh with her. I mean, she doesn't seem sad about it but still.

Ally suddenly stops and holds a hand up in front of me to get me to stop walking, too. I stop, but before I can ask what's up, she proceeds to blow the biggest bubble I have ever seen.

"Whoa!" I say. "It's huge!" Soon, I can't even see her face anymore, just her eyes, getting wider by the second. Finally the whole thing deflates and clings to her face. Ally grimaces.

"Ugh," she says as she peels the sticky pink skin free. "That was cool, right?"

"That was so cool!" I agree, and we continue walking toward the gate.

"We're going to Disneyland this weekend!"

Disneyland?

There's only one thing cooler than that.

"I saw *Cleopatra Jones* with my cousin," I say.

"What's that?" she asks.

"A movie for adults," I say, and can't help but smile.

144

Ally's jaw drops open, revealing the wad of chewing gum lodged high in the back of her mouth.

"Seriously?"

"Uh-huh."

"That is *so* cool," she says. As we approach the gate, Ally waves to her dad, then turns to me. "See you!" She bounds off and throws her arms around him. He swings her up and around like a jitterbug dancer, tosses her in the car, and they're quickly gone.

I run to the gate, expecting to see Mom waiting, but there's no sign of her. Usually she's leaning against the car chatting with another parent. Always on time. But not today.

I guess I shouldn't be surprised.

I loop my fingers through the chain fence that surrounds the playground, watching packs of girls stream out of the gate, arms linked, laughing and singing. Car doors slam shut and one by one, they roll down the hill and away. Soon the curb is completely empty. No cars. No parents. No kids. Just me.

I climb up the gnarly old oak tree just outside the gate. It has a low, wide branch that feels like a couch in a waiting room. Usually it's covered with bodies and I never get a chance to sit on it. But there's no one here now. I plop down and wait.

"Hey there, Stevaroni. What're you still doing here?" says a familiar voice. Mrs. Quakely appears and gives my knee a wiggle. "You the last one standing? Who's coming for you?"

"My mom'll be here." I do a quick scan of Lincoln Boulevard, the main drag, sure she'll turn onto this small side street any second.

"Yeah?" Her teeth are a perfect row of little white Chiclets. "You sure you don't want me to call anybody?"

"No thank you. I'm okay."

She looks out over the streets, too. Together we silently search for a moment before she says, "How you getting along, girlie? I don't ever see you on the handball courts or playing tetherball. Did the principal make you in charge of lookout without telling me? Seems you're always perched up on the jungle gym ready to spot trouble. Is that it? Is that it? Did he make you trouble-spotter? No time for fun and games?"

I laugh and shake my head. "I just...I guess I like being alone," I say, and I can tell right away that she knows that's a lie.

"Well, you're a fun gal, Stevie. But you gotta share some of that fun. Don't hog it all!" She gives me a poke to the ribs, but after a moment more of our scanning the streets and still no sign of Mom, her face falls and gets serious. "If I didn't have to get to barbershop quartet practice, I'd...

Look. You see the bank clock over there?" She points to the large digital sign outside the bank down on Lincoln Boulevard. It blinks the time and then the temperature, then the time again, and so on.

"Yeah, I see it," I say.

"Well, when ten minutes have passed, if your mom still hasn't arrived, I want you to leave this tree and go see Vicky in the office, you hear me? Your mom may have run into a problem getting here. Vicky can call someone and make sure you get home safe, okay?"

"Okay. I will."

"All-righty, friend!" She climbs into her tomato-red Volkswagen Bug—a clown nose of a car—and zooms away.

Car after car turns onto the side street from one direction or the other and I jump every time. But none of them is my mom. Is it possible she forgot?

Then, rolling slowly down the hill, a lone car approaches. It isn't my mom's Pinto but a big blue Cadillac. The very same car that dropped Mom off at home the other night. It slides up along the curb in front of me and stops. Mom quickly exits the passenger side.

"Heya, pumpkin!" she calls, practically jogging up to me. And I notice right away that she isn't wearing a wig. She's wearing her hair out and in a tight natural. I don't think I've ever seen her wear her natural hair out of the house. It's shorter than mine, but it's neat and the sun catches her tiny black curls and makes them glisten.

I can't see around her to catch the face of the mysterious silhouette driving the car, but I have a feeling I know who it'll be.

"I'm so sorry I'm so late. I was having some problems with the Pinto so I asked Clarence for a ride. Remember Clarence?" She leads me to the car and I peer inside.

Clarence.

The man from the library. The man from the phone. Now apparently the man who drives Mom around.

"Hello, Stevie. I hope you don't mind riding in my car. It's a bit of a mess," he rumbles.

"Our car had a flat," Mom says as she motions for me to climb in the back. She takes the front seat and speaks to me from over her shoulder. "I knew something was wrong but didn't realize right away, so they towed it, but turns out the little bit of driving I did on it while it was flat bent the rim. Anyway, it should be ready tomorrow. I'm sorry, pumpkin, but we'll have to take a rain check on the library."

I don't answer. Why did *he* give her a ride? Where is my dad? Why didn't she call him?

Mom gives me a tight smile. She can tell I'm mad. She turns back around, and from the back seat I watch the two of them. The radio oozes out tinny horns and deep thumping beats and is so loud (and their voices so low) that it's hard to hear what they're saying up there. But I do make out his saying, "Your hair looks good like this."

"Yeah?" She blushes and pats her afro.

"Out of sight," he says, and they both chuckle.

I launch assault missiles from my eyes into the back of his big, shiny head.

We reach our apartment building, and Clarence turns to me in the back seat.

"Nice seeing you again, Stevie," he says.

I nod and climb out, but Mom takes a really long time getting out of the car. She and Clarence won't stop talking. Come *on*!

"I'm glad I could be of help," I hear him say before she finally joins me, waving to him as he pulls off. As we approach the front door, we see Naomi there. She's been leaning out and watching us the whole time.

"Hey there," Mom says as she passes her. Naomi says nothing but looks at me and raises an eyebrow.

"Was that the dude from the library?"

I shrug. "Pinto had a flat." But Naomi isn't really interested. She follows after Mom as I watch Clarence's flashy Caddy until it has disappeared completely from our street.

Inside, Naomi has stopped Mom in the living room and is fussing with her hair.

"It looks so good, Aunt Kitty," she says, afro pick in hand, stretching it out and then patting it smooth.

"You think so?" Mom says, reaching back to gently touch her curls. "I feel so . . . naked."

"You should wear it out more. I'm telling you you'll get used to it in no time," Naomi says. She steps in front of Mom and examines her 'fro to be sure it's even all around. "I'll get the name of that oil from Sandra. I can already tell your hair likes it." She stands back from Mom with her hands on her hips and nods.

"It's good?" Mom asks.

"You look fly," Naomi says with a smile.

"Okay. I'll take that as a good thing," Mom says, laughing. Then, "I'm going to make us all something to eat. Would you go up and turn that music down, Naomi? It's way too loud."

"Sorry!"

She quickly heads upstairs. The drapes are open, and Elvis is just outside the sliding glass door, his meow silent from where I stand.

"Hey, you."

I open the door and scoop the cat into my arms, scratch him behind his ears until he purrs.

Elvis and I go up to my parents' room and he cleans himself on the bed while I rummage through the closet.

There's time before dinner. I find a navy turtleneck and a trench coat. Mom's slacks are way too big for me, but a couple of safety pins in the back keep them up. I unbraid my hair and fluff my afro up as high as I can but can't reach the height of Cleopatra Jones's. I line my eyes dramatically, rouge my cheeks and lips. Dangly hoop earrings are the final touch. I hop onto the bed so I can see my full reflection in the mirror over the dresser. Elvis quickly hops off and leaves. But I like what I see!

I aim a karate kick at the mirror, then fall back onto Mom and Dad's bed and stare at a streak of brown water stain that creeps along a corner of the ceiling.

My thoughts turn to Mom and Clarence again. I'm tempted to tell Dad about her new "friend." Maybe he'd make her stop seeing him. But no. He'd get so mad and they would fight. I know it.

I think about what Ally said, about her mom and dad, and how they got divorced. . . . I really don't want that. Maybe if I can talk to my mom, I can convince her to stop hanging out with Clarence. To stop whatever it is that's going on. But if I bring it up, I just know she'll say I'm being nosy again. She'll act like there's nothing strange going on. Unless, maybe I have some sort of evidence.

I roll over and slide the drawer of Mom's bedside table open to look for more clues.

Earplugs, satin eye mask, pennies, Vaseline, hair scarf...

"I made sandwiches!" Mom calls as she heads up the stairs. I quickly slide the drawer shut and roll off, onto the floor and *under* the bed. I watch down the hall as she goes to my room. "Stevie?" Then to Naomi's. "I made sandwiches," she says. "You seen Stevie?" I can't hear Naomi's response, but Mom says, "She's probably playing out back. If you see her, just tell her there's food in the kitchen." She slides into the bathroom near Naomi's room and closes the door.

Hmm. I could just stay here and see if she makes a phone call. Calls Clarence and talks about that secret again, the thing Dad just can't know. But she's bound to catch me under here.

Wait. I have an idea.

I slide out from under the bed and grab a wire clothes hanger and Mom's hand mirror and crack the window of Mom's room open. I duck out as quietly as possible and race to my room before Mom can see me. I push my bedroom window open and reach for the metal rung just outside. A row of rungs starts at the ground level of our building and goes all the way to the roof. They're there in case of a fire. But today, I need to go up on the roof for something else.

Once I'm up there, I tiptoe to where Mom and Dad's

room is, just below, careful not to make any noise that might make Mom look up here. Lying on my back, I twist and turn the wire hanger until it's a long pole, and then I wrap one end tightly around the handle of Mom's hand mirror. I read about how to do this in one of my spy books. The tricky part is getting the angle just right. When I lower it and then look down over the side, it should catch Mom's reflection and bounce it up at me. Maybe I can catch her hiding clues as to what she's been up to.

I think I finally have it right and so I slowly lower the mirror down, but even as it's right next to Mom's window, all I see is blue sky. I quickly pull it back up and adjust the wire. When I lower it now, I see something that looks like Mom's room, but I can't make out what I'm looking at. I think it's her ceiling, or maybe part of her wall.

"Hey!" says a sharp, angry voice directed at *me*. "Hey! What're you doing? Get down from there! Get down from there now before I call the police!"

The police?

I scan the windows of the other apartment buildings and look down at the street. Who is saying that? Where are they? I quickly pull the mirror up and tiptoe to the metal rungs. I climb down and am in my room without ever laying eyes on the busybody who threatened to call the cops on me!

"Ha! Are you supposed to be Cleopatra Jones?" Naomi is passing by my open door. She walks into my room and tugs at my trench, nods approvingly. "Look at my badass cuz!" She laughs and heads downstairs.

Chapter Fifteen

Why a skirt?" Naomi cannot stop laughing. She turns back to the mirror. Black streaks roll down her cheeks. "Oh shoot, Uncle Coop! See what you made me do!"

Dad's legs are neon white. I don't think he's worn shorts since he was seven.

"It's not a skirt," he insists, inspecting the hem of his costume. Mom and Dad are going to a Halloween party. It's the first time in ages that the two of them have gone out together. And I haven't heard them fighting lately. Maybe things are better. Maybe she's stopped seeing Clarence.

"Your legs!" Naomi says. She hovers in front of a small mirror and tries again to apply her eyeliner, but she's laughing so hard the black tears keep coming.

"Oh, cut it out. They're not that bad," he says. "I'm Julius Caesar."

"Hey! We should go together. I'm Cleopatra!" she says.

I hadn't planned on trick-or-treating at all. For the first time ever, I don't have anyone to go with. I tried Jennifer again, but she never called me back. Naomi has Halloween plans of her own though, and that means I have to tag along, like it or not.

Upstairs, Mom is on a call.

"Oh...that's perfect," she says into the receiver, smiling as she adjusts her pixie wig and velvet ears. She catches a glimpse of me in the doorway and hurries off the phone. "Okay. That'd be great. Thank you. Bye."

She hangs up and turns to me.

"Who was tha—?" I start, but she quickly cuts me off.

"You need to get ready, Stevie! Unless you're going without a costume?"

I snatch the Ava from its head and start shoving my hair under it.

"Mom, in your red maxi and your long satin gloves, I could go as Hedy Lamarr!" Without a wig cap and box of bobby pins holding my hair down, the wig keeps fighting me back. I cannot get it to stay down.

"And have you drag the hem all across Santa Monica?"

She doesn't even look up from drawing spiky whiskers across her cheeks.

"We could pin it up!" I insist. But she isn't going for any of it.

"Don't worry, cuz. I got you!" Naomi comes in and sneaks a couple of things from my dad's closet while Mom is caught up painting her cat face.

Naomi drags me to her room. "Shake those pants off." She helps me slip into a humongous pair of men's trousers and cinches the belt tight. My arms swim down the sleeves of an ugly plaid blazer that I have never seen my dad wear. This couldn't possibly be his. Where did she find this?

"Uhhh, what are you dressing me as?"

"Just wait. You're gonna love it!"

Next she goes to town on my makeup but won't let me look.

She grabs the afro pick from her dresser and pulls my afro out big and wide.

"Hey! You're making it too big. Pat it so it's not messy," I say.

"Stop fussing!" she says as she plops a dusty old fedora with a feather tucked in the ribbon on the top. She steps back to inspect her handiwork, tilts the hat a little to one side, and then grins from ear to ear as she walks me to the full-length mirror so I can finally see.

A clown.

No, worse, a hobo. I'm a *hobo*. My disappointed face only makes the costume work better. I'm a *sad* hobo.

The doorbell rings.

"Naomi!" I hear myself whine. And then I remember. "Hey, wait. I can go as Cleopatra Jones. Remember what I had on—"

Dad calls upstairs. "Naomi! Diana Ross and Lieutenant Uhura are down here. Oh, silly me. I'm sorry, it's just Sandra and Denise!"

"I'll be right down!" Naomi shouts, jumping in front of the mirror and playing with her wig, touching up her eyeliner. "We don't have time for you to change, Stevie. I'd have to take off your makeup and—"

"Don't forget my earrings!" Sandra calls up the stairs.

"Bringing them!" shouts Naomi as she starts for her room. But then she stops, gives me the look-over once more. "It's perfect! You look great." And she's gone.

I take a last look in the mirror and I'm convinced my cousin is crazy. I look horrible.

"Hurry up, Stevie! We gotta go!"

Downstairs, Mom is admiring the girls' costumes and they're admiring hers.

"I love the velvet ears and tail!"

"You definitely have the legs for this costume!"

As the girls go back to primping their costumes and touching up their makeup, Dad chimes in. "Yeah, you look good, Kitty," he says, lacing up his gladiator sandals. "I prefer that hair on you. You look very attractive."

I turn to Mom and it's pretty clear that Dad's comment stings. Her hand goes to her wig and as she gives it a small pat, it looks like she's about to say something to him. Maybe tell him how good she feels wearing her hair natural, that she thinks it's also "attractive." But then she stops and turns to Naomi, who's shaking her head and loudly sucking her teeth. Mom lets out a sigh and doesn't say anything to Dad at all. Instead, she goes to the front mirror and drags a final coat of lipstick over her mouth.

"Mom?" I say. "I'm really glad you and Dad are going out. Have a good time."

She laughs a little. "Thanks, pumpkin. You too."

"Ready Stevie?" Naomi's following the girls out the door as they say their goodbyes to my parents. I nod. "Well, let's book!"

The streets are crawling with witches, pirates, and President Nixons.

Every person at every house tells me what a great clown I am. Some even laugh. They're happy to drop candy in my plastic pumpkin. But when they get a load of Naomi and her friends in their clingy costumes, showing lots of leg and sporting some serious cleavage, they hesitate.

They might be a little old for trick-or-treating.

We stop on a corner long enough for me to unwrap a Jolly Rancher and plop it in my mouth. A pair of sheets followed by a plastic-masked Batman pass by.

"You're not tired yet, are you?" Naomi asks me.

"I'm okay." I shrug.

"We're just gonna stop by our friend's place at the top of the hill for a bit and then we can head back."

We're half a block from the house and already I can hear the music thumping. The party is on the second floor of a pink apartment building with big white numbers on the front and matching white railings. The door is wide open and two teenage girls, one dressed as Catwoman and one wearing the shortest, tightest nurse uniform I've ever seen, sit on the stairs smoking cigarettes and sipping from Dixie cups.

This does not look like any kind of Halloween party I've ever been to before.

Naomi hesitates before heading up the stairs.

"Um...maybe you should wait for me here." She hands me her bag of candy and directs me to take a seat on a bottom pebbled step. "You can have my Tootsie Rolls. I won't be long."

I do as I'm told, searching through my candy for an Almond Joy as Naomi, Sandra, and Denise bound up the stairs behind me. I turn to watch them go just in time to see Jimmy emerge from the party in a top hat. He plants a sloppy kiss on Naomi and all I can think of is how her perfect makeup is completely ruined now. They all go inside and I spit out the shard of Jolly Rancher, replacing it with a Reese's Peanut Butter Cup. I slide the whole thing in my mouth and look up to see three girls coming down the sidewalk, about to pass in front of me. The girl with the bare midriff is dressed as Jeannie from the TV show *I Dream of Jeannie*, the one in fishnet stockings (fishnets!), bunny ears, and cotton ball tail is a Playboy Bunny, and the one who's supposed to be Snow White wears a tight corset and her puffy sleeves off her shoulders. As they get closer, I'm shocked to realize that they're all *my* age. And under the rouged cheeks and black wig, I actually recognize Snow White.

It's Jennifer.

Without even thinking, I spring up from the step and run to her.

"Jennifer!" I say through a mouthful of chocolate. But

I'm not sure she recognizes me. She looks at me curiously and turns to the Playboy Bunny. But not just any Playboy Bunny. It's Trina. The naked belly button of Jeannie belongs to Melinda.

"It's me, Stevie," I say, and suddenly realize they're all examining my outfit. Eyebrows raised and silent. They know exactly who I am. It's then that I remember how I'm dressed. I'm a bum. Dad's baggy clothes, clown makeup... and my *hair*! All puffed up. Ugh! All three of them look so... grown-up. Trina and Melinda share amused smiles as they look me up and down. Jennifer avoids my eyes, and as the heat rises in my cheeks, she says nothing. *Nothing.* Finally Trina cuts the silence.

"Why didn't you get a *real* costume, Stevie?" She shakes her head. "I thought you were a boy."

"Oh," I start, trying to find something to say to excuse my appearance, my "boy" look. But I can't think fast enough.

"We have to go," Trina says over her shoulder, already walking.

"Oh, but, Jennifer? My birthday. Let's talk this week, okay? Figure out what we're going to do," I say.

"You know, Stevie, I'm not so sure I'm going to be able to," Jennifer says. She tosses her hair and puffs her princess sleeves. "I've been really busy, and—"

"C'mon, Jennifer." Trina motions to her, then looks at me with her trademark stink face. Jennifer gives me a half smile, then turns and joins the others. As they walk away, I hear an explosion of giggles.

I yank the hat from my head, shove it in my plastic pumpkin on top of the candy, and shake myself free of Dad's scratchy coat. With the sleeves of my shirt, I scrub my face free of as much cartoon vagabond makeup as possible.

Staring into the gray stillness, I try to remember when I was ever mean to Jennifer. Or when I might have made her mad at me. My throat is so tight and the tears come fast and hard. I do all I can to push them back, but they won't stop.

Why doesn't she want to be my friend anymore?

"Hey!" someone calls to me from the stairs, and I turn. It's the sexy nurse. "Forget them!" she says to me before taking a last drag on her smoke and then flicking it down the driveway.

"Seriously!" her cat friend chimes in. "You're better off without those little brats! Girls like them? They're not worth wasting your time on."

There's a sudden roar of laughter from inside the party, and the music cranks up even louder. The two of them turn and trot quickly up the steps, not wanting to miss a minute more of the fun going on inside.

I know they're right. Girls who are mean and who talk behind your back, who make fun of you and make you feel bad about yourself, they're not worth bothering with. I've always known that about Trina and Melinda. And the only reason I've put up with them is because of Jennifer. But I guess I never really realized, until just now, that *Jennifer* is also that kind of girl.

The gray is fast turning to night. Streetlights flicker on. Trick-or-treaters still roam, but they're getting older now. Shouts and cackles can be heard in the distance. In all directions. For many the night has just begun.

"Let's head home!" Naomi appears behind me. Not a trace of lipstick left on her mouth. Her whole face is smiling. That is, until she sees me. Her Cleopatra eyes inspect my tear-streaked cheeks. All clown color wiped away. An even sadder clown than I was when the night began. "Hey, I'm sorry, Stevie. I didn't mean to be gone for so long. That wasn't cool."

"No, it's fine," I say, standing and swiping at the gravel that's clung to my backside. "Really."

I force a smile and do my best to shake Jennifer away.

When we get to the apartment, my parents still aren't back.

"You sure you're not mad at me for leaving you for

so long? You hardly spoke the whole way home." Before we're even in the front door, Naomi's begun peeling away pieces of Cleopatra. Wig, lashes, fancy gold collar.

"I think I'm a little tired," I say, trying to ignore the bad thoughts that keep poking at me.

Naomi exits the bathroom, a bottle of baby oil in one hand and a roll of toilet tissue in the other. She's wiping away all traces of her fancy makeup. "Want to listen to music in my room?"

We head upstairs and quickly sort through our Halloween candy. I pull all the Now and Laters from my bag and toss them into hers, while she tosses anything with nuts into mine.

I never ever get to hang out with Naomi in her room. It's totally off-limits. I haven't even taken a chance on putting her record album back for fear of getting caught in there. So far, seems she hasn't noticed it's gone. Maybe she thinks she left it in Boston.

Her room has transformed since she first arrived a couple of months ago. Hard to imagine it now as a clean white shell, hollow and cold. Today, the floor is a blanket of corduroy, denim, and printed T-shirts. Naomi's clothes are everywhere. Her rainbow-striped book bag is open on the bed, overflowing with folders, books, pencils, and papers.

The blue-and-gold corner of her diary peeks out from under the foot of her bed. But it's her walls I can't get over. There isn't even *one* tiny patch of white wall left. Every inch is covered! Singers, movie stars, a poster of a colorful cobra painted on velvet baring its fangs. A poster of a kitten digging its tiny claws into an overhead branch, trying not to fall. Above him it says, "Hang in There, Baby!" There's a picture of a woman—light-skinned like me—with a big afro. She's speaking to a crowd and isn't all glammed out like Cleopatra Jones. No flashy clothes and not all made up, but she looks confident and strong.

Dangling from a nail holding up the picture of the woman is Naomi's gold necklace with the key to her diary. Man, it is soooo tempting, but I quickly do my best to forget that it's there. I'm already keeping too many secrets!

I spot the picture of Naomi with her mom and dad that I found in her box when she first arrived. It's tacked to the wall and Naomi has drawn hearts on the wall all around it (she'd better not let my mom see that!). Naomi looks so happy in the photo. Even Auntie Florence, who's barely smiling, looks content. We have a similar picture. From a trip to Palm Springs we took a couple of years ago. We stopped to get date shakes on the way home and Mom asked a lady in a big red-and-white muumuu dress if she could take our picture. My dad hates having his picture taken, but he did it anyway. Couldn't get him to smile, but at least we got him to pose with us. Mom and I turned on big cheesy smiles that reflected what a fun time we were having that day. And Dad, like Auntie Florence, even without a smile, still looked content.

"Do you miss him?" I turn to Naomi. And when she looks up from her magazine and sees what I'm referring to, her cheeks fall flat and her eyes look bigger and browner than ever.

After a moment she takes a deep breath and says, "Every. Single. Day." Then she quickly buries her face in the magazine again.

"Naomi?" I'm thinking maybe now is as good a time as any to ask her what *she* thinks about my mom's strange behavior. She might even have some answers, seeing as she's older and probably knows about these things. "You think it's weird that my mom is out doing something *all* the time? You know, always running errands? Always going grocery shopping or doing things for Mona?"

"What do you mean? You rather she *didn't* get groceries? I don't think so." She laughs to herself.

"But I mean she *always* seems to be off doing something," I say.

Naomi puts down her magazine and looks at me. "I don't know what you're getting at, Stevie. Your mom has stuff she needs to do. What's the big deal?"

"Well, I don't know, I mean..." I'm not exactly sure how to start. "Remember when we saw her at the library talking to that guy? The bald guy?" I ask.

"Clarence...yeah." She shrugs.

"And then he drove me and her home that one day? Remember?" I lean in toward her and raise my eyebrows, hoping she'll get where I'm going, but she just raises her eyebrows back. "And you see how she's wearing her hair these days?"

"Natural? I like it," Naomi says, and closes her magazine.

"I do too, but...I think she changed her hair—and even her clothes—for *him*, I think—"

"Stevie, what are you—?"

"I think Clarence is her boyfriend," I blurt, and even I'm surprised. I mean, I've been thinking she spends too much time with him and wondering what all this secretive stuff is, stuff she can't tell my dad, but now that I've heard the words come out of my mouth, the possibility, for the first time, seems real.

Naomi looks at me with her mouth open but totally

silent for a moment before letting out a sharp "Ha!" and going right back to her magazine. Shaking her head and flipping pages, she says, "Girl! You need to stop. He isn't your mom's boyfriend."

My face is hot as coals and my stomach's tying itself in knots. I have a rush of feeling silly. I should never have said anything to Naomi. She thinks I'm just a dumb kid. But I have spy blood. I know I'm right.

"She didn't used to be gone so much," I press, but Naomi's still shaking her head and not even looking at me. "And now she's *always* out. I know it's with him. You saw them in the library!"

"That don't mean nothing, Stevie. Don't tell me you're as old-fashioned as your dad," she says. "Men and women can be friends. There's nothing wrong with that."

"But she's changing! Her hair, her clothes..."

"I changed *my* hair. Heck! I didn't do it for no man," she says. "And neither did your mom. She did it for herself."

"But she's keeping secrets from my dad. That has to mean—"

"Look, Stevie. I like your dad—I do. But we both know that he would get all weird and jealous if he knew anything about your mom having a friend in Clarence. He'd be jumping to conclusions, just like you are!" She shakes her head and goes back to her magazine. "Just lay off your mom. Please? She's got so much on her plate. The last thing she needs is you accusing her of crazy stuff. Let's just drop it, okay?"

I'm still not convinced Naomi's right, but what she's saying does kind of make sense. Could I really be wrong?

"Okay," I say.

Neither of us noticed the song end, and we sit there with only the sound of the needle skipping for a while before Naomi realizes, hops up, and shakes free a new album.

I try to forget the conversation and go back to admiring the patchwork of images on her walls.

"I like your room," I say. "I'd love to decorate my club-house like this."

She makes herself comfy on her bed again, propping her head and shoulders up by what looks like all the pillows in the house.

I point to the row of albums leaning against the wall.

"Can I look?" I ask.

"What you wanna hear?" Naomi doesn't look up as she asks. She's still squinting into the magazine.

"Oh, I don't know. I don't mind." I jump down to the albums and flip through some, but I don't know any of them. Wouldn't know what to choose. But then I see another album with the singer I saw on Naomi's first day here. The one from the album I took. *The one that's still hidden under my mattress.* This time the other band members each have a tiny picture in the four corners of the album, but Chaka Khan is dead in the center, sitting on a red couch shaped like lips. Her arms and legs are stretched out wide. Feathers hang from clips all throughout her hair.

Her hair! It's so big. Like her smile.

Mona, Florence, and even Mom would not approve. The first day of Mom's Barbizon model training she was taught to always keep your legs crossed, usually at the ankle, and hands neatly in your lap. Chaka would be a big FAIL.

But she'd definitely get an A+ on that smile.

"This one!" I hold it up to Naomi. She looks up from the magazine, leaps to her feet, and proceeds to put it on.

"I think there's another one by this band in that stack," she says, handing me the record cover and then plopping back down onto the bed with her magazine.

Oh good! She still hasn't noticed it's missing.

The music is booming and so is Chaka. It's like she's emptying her soul into the atmosphere. She roars pure joy and thunder.

"You like this?" Naomi asks again, not looking up.

"I do!"

Naomi cranks the music even louder, then hops up on

her bed and pretends to sing into an imaginary microphone the way Jennifer and I used to.

"C'mon, Stevie!"

I jump up and join in, dancing and stomping all over Naomi's clothes and school papers. I grab a Magic Marker for a microphone and do my best to sing along. I sing loud. I roar like Chaka.

And for the first time in so long, I'm truly having fun.

Chapter Sixteen

Angry voices cut through my sleep. It's my parents in the kitchen.

"Well, you got just what you wanted, didn't you?"

"Stop it, Coop!"

Ugh, not again. I haven't heard them fight like this in a while. And I don't think Naomi has *ever* heard them fight like this—and I don't want her to. I step into the dark hall. Maybe I can go down and stop them. Or at least quiet them.

"Got yourself a babysitter so you can be free to run around with your boyfriend!"

I stop in my tracks.

Boyfriend?

Then, suddenly, I feel Naomi behind me in the hall. I turn to her and she just shakes her head.

"Poor Aunt Kitty," she whispers. "You go back to your room, Stevie. This doesn't concern you."

I nod, and Naomi goes back into her room, closing the door behind her.

But I have no intention of just listening to them like this. I drag my feet down the hall, following the voices. As I arrive at the bottom of the stairs, wondering what I can say or do to make them stop fighting, the shouting suddenly stops and is replaced by the shuffle of Mom's slippers hurrying across the carpet. She fusses under her breath. I can't make out what she's saying but I know she's cursing my dad.

"Oh!" she gasps when she sees me. "Stevie! You scared me. What're you trying to do, give me a heart attack?"

"I heard you guys fighting. It woke me up," I say. "Are you okay?"

"Yeah, pumpkin. I'm okay." She drapes an arm around my shoulders and leads me up the stairs and to my bed.

Mom's still in her cat costume, but most of her makeup has been cried away. She's all puffy eyes and nose. Pink, swollen lips.

She tucks my blanket in around my chin and shoulders over and over again.

"You know how much I love you, don't you?" She tries to smile, but tears fill her eyes and she quickly closes them.

I think she's about to come clean. To tell me everything. About how Clarence *is* her boyfriend. That she's so sorry for having lied all this time. That if I really want her to, she'll call the whole thing off and we can go back to the way things used to be. But instead, she tucks me in even tighter and I'm afraid I could have an accident trying to get out of here to use the bathroom in the night.

"Mom, are you sure you're okay?"

She nods. Pulls her cat ears free.

"Hey, you still haven't told me what kind of cake you want for your birthday. It's almost here!" She forces a giggle as she attempts to tickle my mummified torso.

"Oh, I don't know," I say as Mom begins unhooking the skinny bobby pins that keep her pixie wig in place. "I think I like vanilla." She lifts the wig from her head.

"That sounds good," she says. But as she drags her pointy nails through her coarse hair, combing it until it's nice and neat, it feels like she's elsewhere. Not really talking to me. Not thinking about cake.

"Go to sleep, pumpkin," she says as she rises.

Then she walks to the door, pauses, and drops the pixie straight in the trash.

Chapter Seventeen

Mrs. Quakely loves birthdays. On those special days, we come back from lunch and she's turned all the lights out. The room is dark except for a cake covered in lit candles: one for every year of the birthday person's life. Everyone's giddy and excited. It's a celebration. And everybody knows there's no schoolwork during a celebration.

On top of that, we get cake.

We enter the room and edge up to the table that holds the cake. Usually everybody nudges and teases the birthday person. They tickle them and elbow them and threaten to spank them for every year.

But today it's *my* birthday.

No one scoots up close to me and shares a giggle. There's

no tickling. The class gathers and whispers and I can hear them asking each other whose day it is.

Mrs. Quakely walks around behind us, carrying the birthday crown. Everyone watches intently, eager to find out who we're all supposed to sing to. Who's going to blow out the candles. When she stops behind me, Kenny and Donald hoot and holler. Mrs. Quakely shoots them a look, and they quickly muffle their laughs.

I know my face is scarlet. My cheeks are so hot. I'm sure they're about to explode into flames. Everyone is staring at me, and I swear there's a low patter of snickering whirling round the table. The song hasn't even begun.

As Mrs. Quakely's lumbering torso hovers over my back, I feel her left arm go up behind me, conducting the class to begin.

"Happy birthday to you.

Happy birthday to you.

Happy birthday, dear..."

I know what's coming next.

"Char-min!"

Okay, so not *everybody* says it, but a good half of the class does.

"Happy birthday to you!"

And now, for the worst part.

You see, this morning, after my mom and Naomi had sung me happy birthday and we'd had our special breakfast, I was sitting on the kitchen chair waiting to get my hair braided, like always. Then Naomi asked, "Why don't you wear your hair *out* today? Wear your natural? It is, after all, *your* day." At first I was ready to protest. Was she crazy? Didn't she know how I felt about being the only one in the whole school with that big puff on my head? How I stick out like a big, fuzzy sore thumb? So big and wide even the *Skylab* Space Station could see it.

But she *did* know. I'd told her about the teasing and why Mom and I got up early every day so we would have time to weave my 'fro into two obedient braids. She knew how I felt and she was saying to wear it anyway.

I thought about it long and hard. I imagined Kenny and Donald and all those other crusty-fingered morons digging in my hair. I thought of the toilet paper chant that came whether my hair was out or braided. I saw Jennifer's look on Halloween. And then I thought about Chaka Khan and her smile. Hair out and wild, she was entirely herself and free. I thought about Cleopatra Jones, kickin' butt in all her gorgeousness, her big afro filling the silver screen. The cool lady from Naomi's wall. And I thought about Mom. No wig this morning again. Picking out her natural with Naomi's plastic comb that has a Black Power fist for a handle.

She was right. Today is *my* day. I'm twelve today. No more hiding behind little-girl braids.

"Okay," I finally said, and turned to Mom. "Let's go for it."

I walked into the classroom with my chin high. I was ready for the chants. I was ready to block whoever put their hands in my hair without asking. And for the most part, the morning had gone okay.

But I'd forgotten about the birthday crown.

After a few kids tag on, "And many more!" I feel Mrs. Quakely hesitate over the top of me before she attempts to place the birthday crown on my head. In her hesitation, a wave of giggles ripples through the class as they all realize *that* crown and *that* hair are not likely friends. I can practically hear the gears in Mrs. Quakely's brain turning as she asks herself *How on earth do I do this?*

And then, I feel something in my hair. Not the crown, but fingers. Mrs. Quakely's fingers are in my hair, making little parts in my afro. She's trying to make a path for the crown to settle into. But as she lowers the golden cardboard, my hair flings it out like a spring-coiled toy. Her fingers fight back and she's quickly in there again pushing and parting. The giggles have turned to squeals of laughter. I look down at my desk. I can feel the tears threatening.

"Hush!" Mrs. Quakely snaps, and then, finally, she lets go of the fancy hat and it stays put. I feel her take one careful step back, a moment of held breath, before she can be sure she's defeated the powerful 'fro. Satisfied that I've been properly crowned, she takes me by the shoulders and whispers loudly in my ear, "Happy birthday, Stevie!"

I close my eyes and shut out the grinning faces, the hands covering mouths. I ignore the snickering. I think hard on my wish.

I wish I had a friend.

I open my eyes and the first person I see is Ally. She's looking directly at me and smiling. She looks genuinely happy for me. That it's my birthday. For a moment, the brilliant, twinkling flames before me promise a brand-new year full of good things. I feel a rush of happiness, just before I bend forward to blow them out. But as I lean in, the crown topples from my head and onto the cake. Onto the candles. The flammable paint ignites, and my twinkling candles turn fast into a blaze. Everyone jumps back from the table shrieking, and within seconds Mrs. Quakely has enlisted the help of the trusty fire extinguisher to put out the fire and any birthday joy.

Back at home, there's no one there to wish me a happy birthday. Sure, Mom said it this morning, and so did Naomi. And they'll be back soon. But I need them here *now* so their birthday love can cleanse me of today's stench.

Dad was already out of the house when I came down for breakfast, but Mom assured me that we'd all have my celebration together tonight after dinner. I guess I'll have to be patient. I can do that. There'll be more cake. There'll even be a present or two. And maybe Mom and Dad can get along—they've barely spoken since the big fight on Halloween.

Sipping Dr Pepper through a Krazy Straw, I head down to my clubhouse. I study the walls. I'm going to finally decorate this place. Clean it up and get rid of all this dust. Start an official club. That'll mean coming up with a good name and maybe even a theme. I'll ask Mom if I can get a poster or two. Maybe Naomi has something cool that she'd let me have. And even though Naomi's older, she could still be in my club. I'd even let Jimmy in if she wanted. Maybe I'll ask Ally to join, too.

I get a pit in my stomach thinking about how Jennifer won't be calling me for my birthday. Why should I even care that she doesn't want to be my friend anymore? If she wants to spend her time with mean girls like Trina and Melinda, so be it. Besides, they probably have some dumb girly-girl club with stupid code names like Cinderella, Snow White, and Sleeping Beauty. They probably sit around all day talking about boys and fingernail polish. I hate them.

Upstairs, the front door opens and closes hard. I recognize Naomi's stomping. First to the bathroom, then shortly after, to the kitchen.

The phone rings upstairs and Naomi stomps to it. I hear the low mumble of her hello.

And then, downstairs in my hideout, I hear:

Click.

I sit up straight and look into the tunnel. The sound definitely came from down here, but there's nothing in the tunnel. No recorder. My dad took it. My eyes scan every inch of wall, of floor, ceiling…nothing. But I'm sure I heard it.

Through the floorboards above, I hear what I'm pretty sure is Naomi saying, "Okay. Bye."

Click.

There it is again. I think it came from behind me, but there's nothing there…except…I stand and walk over to the giant water heater in the corner of the room. Just behind it, lying on the dusty floor, is the gray box. The recorder. A black cord attached to its rear snakes along the wall to the ceiling, where tiny silver staples secure it in place. The cord travels all the way to the tunnel. To the phone box marked "5."

Has it been here all this time? Did he just move it here? I really want to listen to the tape. To see if maybe Mom's on there talking to Clarence, revealing her secret. Is he really her boyfriend, like Dad thinks? What's so important that he'd be as sneaky as this? But I don't dare reach for the recorder this time. Today, crisscrossed in front of the recorder, wrapped around the two water heaters, are skinny yards of my mom's sewing thread. And between the threads, way off on either side, near the heaters and easy to miss if you're not as perceptive as a person with spy blood, are two spoons so precariously woven in that the slightest disruption would send both spoons to the floor, making it clear that someone had discovered the recorder—that someone was onto Dad and *his* secret.

Mom got a cake. Vanilla cake with vanilla frosting, colorful sprinkles all over the top and sides. In red handwriting it says: *Happy Birthday!* I count twelve candles.

"*...happy birthday to you!*"

I take a deep breath, blow out the candles, and wish for friends...again. Everyone claps and cheers. Mom gives me a kiss on the cheek. Naomi high-fives me. Dad threatens to spank me twelve times. The cake is delicious. I have two slices.

"Okay, Stevie, I think it's opening-presents time!" Mom says, and directs everyone to the living room, where a stack of colorful boxed gifts awaits me.

As I walk down the hall and pass the mirror there, I catch a glimpse of myself and smile. I reach up to straighten my pointy party hat, which sits perfectly atop the smooth and silky Ava wig.

Chapter Eighteen

Look at that fat orange streak," Naomi says. She points like the sky is a blackboard and she's teaching astronomy to the class.

We're sitting on the hood of Jimmy's Camaro watching the sunset from the Santa Monica beach parking lot.

"But the rest of it is purple," I say.

Even when the yolk of sun has dipped and disappeared into the Pacific, we all still stare, transfixed, unable to move, hypnotized by the beauty of it all.

Jimmy finally breaks the spell.

"All right, y'all," he says, walking to the driver's seat and motioning for us to get in, too. "It's belated birthday burger night!"

Ever since Jimmy heard about my birthday disaster at

school, about the crown on fire and soggy cake, he's been talking about taking a trip to Tom's #5.

"You know, for me, it's not really my birthday until I've had a Tom's number five chiliburger," he said. "I think my dad got me hooked on that tradition."

"Chili on a burger?" I asked.

"That don't sound right!" Naomi shook her head and squirmed.

But Jimmy insisted, and tonight we'll find out for ourselves.

"Get in the car," he calls from behind the steering wheel. "Let's go!"

We find a table around the side of the burger stand and plant ourselves, licking smoky chili from the oozing sides of the burgers and from our fingers.

"Oh my God," Naomi purrs. "This is *so* good!"

"What'd I say?" Jimmy laughs. "Stevie? What do you say, little cuz?"

Both of my cheeks are stretched full of delicious burger, so all I can do is nod and give him a big thumbs-up.

"That's what I'm saying!" He takes another chomp and half his burger is gone.

We climb back into the car and are still wiping the dark orange oil from our hands and chins when a black-and-white police car's siren chirps once and the officer driving pulls up directly behind the Camaro.

"Oh man," Jimmy says under his breath.

"What the hell does he want?" Naomi frowns as she swivels to watch the officer exit his car and walk to Jimmy's window.

When I was little, I remember Officer Bill coming to visit my class. He stood at the front of the room in his dark blue uniform, policeman's badge gleaming on his chest. He told us that police officers are our friends and are there to help us when we need it. He told us jokes and made us all laugh. But that was the only time I ever saw a policeman up close.

"How're you doing, Officer?" Jimmy's tone is friendly and somehow that seems to anger Naomi. She sucks her teeth and turns to look out the passenger window at absolutely nothing.

The police officer is tall and wide, and the crisp white shirt of his uniform is stretched tight across his chest. His name plate reads "McMillan." He's got a mustache that's so fat it looks like our class hamster took a nap under his nose. He's pulled the dark visor of his cap completely over his eyebrows. I can't see his eyes at all.

"License and registration," he says without an ounce of emotion. No "I'm doing fine" or "I could be better, you?" Like he was some kind of robot. And he must be four feet from the car. Why can't he come a little closer?

I turn and look at the Tom's #5 window, at the tables

outside. Sure enough, people are watching. Whispering. I wonder if they're thinking that Jimmy did something bad. Like he's wanted for robbery or something.

Jimmy takes his license and some papers from behind the car visor and hands them to the officer, who takes one long step toward the car to retrieve them.

"What's the trouble, sir?" Jimmy asks. But he's quickly silenced with a single palm held up to say STOP.

Naomi is shifting in her seat from side to side, still sucking her teeth, like she just ate a bucket of ribs. Finally she leans over Jimmy and barks at the officer.

"He didn't do nothing. We *just* got in the car. We were just at—"

"Ma'am, please sit back," the robot man says.

"The car isn't even *on*," Naomi says, tight-lipped and nose flared.

"Ma'am." The stop sign hand goes up again, and this time Naomi stops talking and huffs back into her seat.

Jimmy hasn't once taken his eyes off the officer but finally turns his head to Naomi and whispers, "It's okay."

Naomi's nervousness, the cold police officer, and Jimmy's trying to calm Naomi down (from what?) has set my heart pounding. I'm beginning to wonder if maybe Jimmy *is* in some sort of trouble. Maybe he's wrong and things *aren't* okay.

The officer takes a step forward, bends at the waist, and looks into the car. His eyes travel to Naomi and along the seats of the car. Then he turns to the back seat. To me.

"Who is this?" He points to me as he asks Jimmy, and I feel my whole body go cold.

"That's my cousin. Stevie Morrison," Jimmy answers. And while it feels kind of nice to hear Jimmy call me his cousin, I'm not sure why he lied.

He continues to scan the back of the car but stops when he sees the stack of Black Panthers flyers on the floor. Even with his eyes mostly shielded from view, I see his deep frown.

"Please step out of the vehicle," he says, stepping back to his four-feet line.

"Get out? Why?" Naomi looks more helpless than I've ever seen her as she watches Jimmy open his door and exit the car. "I can't believe this crap," she mutters, and I quickly turn to the officer to be sure he didn't hear her. But when I turn back to Naomi, still mumbling under her breath, I hear less bite in her voice. Less anger. And I think maybe she's trembling.

The officer makes Jimmy face the car and put both hands on the hood. He pats his arms, his chest, his waist, and all the way down his legs before finally telling him to put his hands behind his back.

"Oh no," I hear myself say as the glare of the streetlight on the handcuffs cuts my eyes.

"What?" Before Naomi can fully grasp what's happening, she's flung her door open and is circling the back of the car to Jimmy and Officer Robot. "Jimmy!"

"Ma'am, please return to the vehicle," the officer says.

"It's okay, Naomi," says Jimmy. "Get back in the car. Stevie, don't you move."

I want to call to her, tell her to get back here. But I'm scared to make a move. I've never been in a situation like this and I'm afraid the officer will get mad if I speak. That I could make matters worse.

"Ask anyone at Tom's," Naomi says, and points to the food counter. "We've been there. Just left. He ain't done a damned—"

"Back in the car, *now*," the officer barks, his voice hard and unflinching as he holds Jimmy's head down against the side of the car.

But Naomi doesn't come back to the car. She heads right toward them, begging the officer now to let Jimmy go. Insisting he did nothing wrong.

By the time she reaches the two of them, the officer has pulled Jimmy away from the side of the Camaro by his arm and is heading for the patrol car. Passing Naomi, he lifts the STOP hand again, but this time she's so close to him that his hand connects with her jaw, her head jerks back, and she loses her footing and falls.

"Naomi!" I shout without even meaning to. I can't see if she's okay.

"Ma'am," says the robot. "I need you to get back into the car." He looks at her there in the road, but she's silent. Doesn't say a word. Neither does Jimmy. I don't understand the sudden silence until I follow both of their gazes and see for the first time that though his left hand grips Jimmy's arm, the officer's right hand rests on the handle of the gun on his hip.

Naomi slides back to the curb, then is finally on her feet and back in the front seat.

"Are you okay?" I whisper, but she doesn't answer. I turn, and through the back window we watch the officer lean Jimmy against the side of his squad car while he speaks into a radio.

It's about an hour before Jimmy is finally allowed back in the Camaro.

Jimmy waits until after the cop has disappeared into the dark night, completely out of sight, before finally speaking.

"Seems I fit the description of a prowler in the neighborhood." He looks straight ahead as though he could still see the officer. As though he's still measuring his words and movements, careful not to invite more trouble.

Naomi slides to him and wraps her arms around him, and they're silent and still for a while before he pulls away from her and studies her jaw and face for any indication of harm.

"I'm okay," she says.

He swings around to me.

"Oh, little cuz," he says, eyes full of concern. "I'm so sorry you had to see that."

"No, I—" I don't know what to say, so I echo Naomi. "I'm okay."

We glide through the streets without the radio. Without a word. Arriving home far later than we meant to, but that doesn't really matter.

Mom's still not there.

Chapter Nineteen

Of course it matters when you get home. It's Thanksgiving....But you said you were bringing the turkey. I should've already put it in....What do you mean you didn't get it? Coop!"

"Well, I can see your father hasn't changed much," says Aunt Florence. She chuckles to herself and shakes her head. She came clear across the country for Thanksgiving and it looks like there won't be turkey.

Mom hangs up and turns to Florence and me. Takes a deep, exasperated breath and lets it out hard.

"I don't know what to do with him," Mom says. "Can you imagine if *I* forgot something like that? If *I* didn't do what I'd promised?"

"Don't worry about it. We'll figure something else out."

"Oh, it's not just that, it's..." Mom shakes her head and sucks her teeth. "But yes, Flo! You came all this way and I can't even give you a proper Thanksgiving—"

"Kitty, stop it! You know I didn't come out here for turkey and stuffing!"

"Yes, but...oh, he makes me so mad."

"If I remember correctly, Coop's always been one for getting distracted. For forgetting things. But Kitty, you have you a good man there. A good provider. Try not to be so hard on him."

The doorbell rings.

"That's Mona!" I say, and jump to answer the door. As I run through the living room, I pass Naomi on her way to the kitchen. "No turkey today!" I announce.

"What?" she says, then continues to the kitchen. "No turkey?" I hear her whine.

Mona barrels past me and peels off her coat without her usual warm smiles and requests for kisses.

"I have had the morning from hell, and there was no way I was gonna even attempt to pull a pie outta my hat, so Kitty might be sore, but there was no way! Not today. Heck, I'll go get a Hostess something-or-other from the corner store. We'll make do."

She finally stops long enough to take me in.

"Hey, pretty girl! What's wrong with you? Where's my sugar?" I go in for a squeeze and a smooch, and when she releases me, all bright and smiling face, I say, "No turkey today."

Her smile falls to the floor.

"What?" She marches to the kitchen and I hang on her tail. "You mean to tell me that boy didn't come through with the *bird*?"

Mom shakes her head sadly, then, inspecting Mona's empty hands, asks, "Where's my pie?"

"We'll get some cookies at the store," she says as she bends and wraps her arms around Florence. "Lookie who's here!" She rocks her back and forth, which makes Florence giggle like a schoolgirl.

"What're we going to do?" asks Naomi, borderline pouting. She's been talking about turkey all week. Honestly, I don't see what the big deal is. It's always dry, but everyone always says it's not. Like it's so special. Like it's better than chicken, when it's not!

"I'm gonna run out and see if I can't find something," Mom says, heading for the living room. "Mona, you come with me. You all watch the parade."

I love the Macy's Thanksgiving Day Parade. The huge floats, movie and TV stars.

"I hope Underdog shows up," I say.

"I'm sure he will," says Florence. "Seems like he always does."

Aunt Flo only arrived yesterday, but before that first day was even over, she and Naomi got into it.

"These people are taking good care of you, giving you food, a place to stay, and you can't even be respectful enough to keep this room in order?"

"I didn't *ask* to come all the way out here!"

"It's embarrassing, Naomi. Like I didn't raise you right."

I probably didn't even *need* to hold the water glass up against the wall to hear them, but I did it anyway.

Today they seem to have mellowed out.

"I do not miss having to wear my big ol' winter coat," says Auntie Flo, pointing at the New York crowd bundled in hats and mittens. "Look at her huge coat. I can practically see her teeth chattering."

"Can you imagine having to be out in that cold all day?" Naomi says, and shakes her head.

"And smiling?" Aunt Flo says, laughing.

"Is it *that* cold?" I ask.

"It is to *me*," says Aunt Flo. "But then, I'm not from cold weather country originally. You know, your mom and I grew up in South Carolina. It never got that cold there."

"My dad loves the cold," I tell her.

"Oh, now, see. That's 'cause he's from Montana. He grew up in the cold," says Aunt Florence.

"But my uncle Owen moves around in his van to *avoid* the cold, and he grew up in Montana, too," I remind her.

"Yeah, well, Owen's always been...well, different," she says, and laughs.

I've never thought of my uncle Owen as "different." He's one of the nicest people I've ever known. Always nice to everyone. Sure, he lives in his van, but...

"Like how?" I ask.

"Oh, never mind," she says, swatting a hand at the air like she's trying to dodge a fly.

"Does Uncle Coop have any other brothers or sisters?" Naomi asks.

"Yeah," I say. "He has two sisters."

"They ain't gonna come down for the holiday? For Christmas maybe?"

"Oh, don't count on that!" Flo says, her laugh becoming a bit of a cackle.

"Why not?" Naomi frowns and turns away from the TV so she can face her mom. "There a problem?"

Flo stammers some. Her laugh has a nervous edge. "No. No problem."

"Then what?" Naomi's gaze is piercing, and Aunt Flo seems to be avoiding laser burn when she tries to direct Naomi's eyes back to the TV.

"Look, it's Lola Falana," she says, smiling at the set.

But Naomi isn't interested.

"Stevie, you ever even met your other aunties? On your dad's side?" Naomi asks me.

"No. We have pictures." I run to the photo albums and quickly flip open to the pages of black-and-white photos. Of my dad and his sisters when they were my age. To photos of them all older, both of my aunts with husbands. There are pictures of them with Owen. And when the pictures become color, I notice for the first time that my dad isn't in any of them. And while I don't expect there to be any with them holding me as a baby, I realize for the first time that there aren't any pictures of my aunts with my mother, either.

"Is there a reason they don't visit? Why Stevie hasn't met them?" Naomi asks her mom pointedly.

"Oh, now, don't go getting me into trouble," Aunt Flo says, and turns to me. "It's nothing, Stevie. Just some folks get stuck in their ways. Not bad people, just not used to change."

Just as I'm trying to wrap my head around what kind

of "change" Aunt Florence could be talking about, Naomi chimes in again.

"You mean to tell me they have a problem with Uncle Coop marrying a sister?"

"I—I don't think it's as simple as—as that," says Aunt Florence, the stammer returning to her speech.

"But it sounds like it is," says Naomi. "Pretty simple."

"Do you have to make trouble, Naomi?"

"I'm not!" Naomi huffs. "'Cause I'm interested in the *truth*, I'm trouble?"

Aunt Flo shakes her head and turns from Naomi's hot gaze.

"Let's have a good time," she says. "It's Thanksgiving."

And that's when I realize that a "bad" time would be going down the path Naomi started down. Probably to get to the truth as to why my dad's sisters and their families never come around. It's something I've never given a lot of thought to until now. And I think I know what Naomi is getting at. I think she's pretty sure it has something to do with my mom's being Black.

I wrack my brain for a time when one of them called the house or maybe visited when I was little. Maybe I've just forgotten. Think, think.

But I come up empty.

I hear Aunt Flo's words over again: "*Some folks get stuck in their ways. . . . Just not used to change.*"

Naomi drops the whole subject and heads upstairs.

"Whatever," she says. "I'll be right back!"

Florence settles on the couch.

"Don't mind any of that, Stevie. You hear me?" she says, then turns to the TV. "Oh, look, Stevie! It's Underdog!"

In a flash, Naomi is bounding into the living room with a jar of something green in her hand.

"Mom, will you braid my hair?"

I sit on the arm of the couch and watch. I can't even follow the parade anymore. I'm too hypnotized by Aunt Flo's precision braiding technique. In awe of the pristine rows along Naomi's scalp.

"It's really not that hard, Stevie. You could do it. Want to try?" she asks, winking at me and smiling in anticipation of Naomi's reaction.

"Oh no, no, no!" Naomi calls from the floor between her mom's knees. Aunt Flo and I crack up.

"Stop pulling away, Naomi. I'm only playing." She returns to weaving one oiled section of hair over the other. "But you might want to teach Stevie sometime."

"Okay," Naomi says. "You want me to?"

I nod like crazy even though Naomi can't see me. "That'd be cool!" I say.

I hear two sets of shoes approaching the front door and Mona talking loud and fast. Before Mom can get the key in the lock, I'm up and opening it for them.

"What did you get?" I ask.

"Ooh! Thanks, pumpkin," says Mom.

"We weren't the only ones out there hitting the streets for alternative dinners! You should've seen the line at Kentucky Fried Chicken!"

"Did you really? Kentucky Fried?" Aunt Flo says as she braids the tip of the last braid down to its very end and pats Naomi's shoulders. "All done."

"Thanks, Mom!" Naomi jumps up, gently touching her bumpy braids. "You couldn't find turkey?"

"I like Kentucky Fried better anyway!" I say, grabbing the big bucket of chicken from Mom and heading to the kitchen.

"And they even had pie!" Mom says, holding up two more bags loaded with dessert.

We shake the tablecloth open and set the table. Mom puts the chicken on a serving plate, covers it with foil, and places it dead center of the table. If you didn't know better, you'd swear there was turkey.

Mom tells us to all take a seat, that Dad and Owen won't be back for hours and we're not waiting. I don't argue. The smell of the colonel's special seasonings is making my mouth water.

"I can't wait to meet your friend Sandra," says Aunt Flo.

"You'll like her," Naomi says. "She's cool. We usually hang out at her place after school."

"Well, I'm happy to hear you're keeping yourself out of trouble," says Flo. "Did you hear about Memphis? You can't go getting these police officers angry, Naomi."

"I know," Naomi says, and sighs.

"And that boy wasn't even near that officer. He was climbing a fence." Aunt Florence shakes her head and serves herself mashed potatoes from the Styrofoam container. "Got to be real careful."

"What boy?" I ask. "What happened to him?"

"They shot him," Naomi says, biting into a drumstick.

Mom, Aunt Florence, and even Aunt Mona all quickly descend on Naomi.

"What's wrong with you?"

"You'll scare her!"

"There's more to it than—"

Naomi tosses the bone onto her plate and turns to face her mother.

"I don't know what's wrong with y'all. I didn't say anything that wasn't true. Stevie can handle the truth." She turns to me. "Right?"

I nod, but I am still trying to understand. He was climbing a fence and the officer *shot* him? But *why*?

"Stevie, pumpkin, I don't want you getting yourself worried about this stuff," Mom says. "It was a terrible thing that happened, but it's nothing for *you* to worry about. You hear me?"

Again I nod, but my mind travels to Jimmy and the policeman who stopped him. Who stopped all of us. About the gun in his holster. How he put his hand on it. *Was he thinking about shooting Jimmy? Would he have shot me?*

"Look, Mom," Naomi says. "I'm not causing any kind of trouble and I don't have any reason to be talking to the cops, so you don't need to be getting all bent outta shape."

I'm still frozen. If Naomi hadn't stopped when the officer told her to, would he have pulled his gun free and fired?

I feel a strange pull on me from across the table, and when I look up, it's Mom. She's not talking to Flo or Naomi, she's just looking at me. When I meet her eyes, she frowns as if to say, "What's wrong?" I quickly shake myself away from thoughts of Jimmy and the robot police officer. Of Naomi struck and falling to the ground. Of a hand on a gun. A warning.

I force a grin at Mom and quickly dart my eyes away,

trying to engage in the conversation swirling around us. It's already changed from the police. Mona's talking about Southern barbecue.

"I don't care how much you season it, the chicken in the South is gonna taste better simply 'cause the soil is better, so the feed that fattens the bird is better. You are what you eat and all that."

Once dinner's done, Mom ushers everyone out of the kitchen.

"Stevie and I will join you after we've cleaned up in here."

Mom washes. I dry. But we aren't silent for long.

"That police talk seemed to get you upset," she says. "But that boy didn't stop when the officer told him to. If you're staying out of trouble, if you're behaving yourself, you have nothing to worry about."

"So, you mean an officer shouldn't stop you if you haven't done anything wrong?"

"That's right."

"And if he calls to you and you answer, he should just leave you alone?"

"What's going on, Stevie?" She dries her hands on a nearby dish towel and takes me by the shoulders. "I'm sorry all that talk about that boy scared you, pumpkin, but you have nothing to worry about. You're never gonna have any kind of run-in with the police. I'm sure of it."

She wraps her arms around me and gives me a squeeze.

"C'mon," she says. "Let's go see what they're up to in there."

I follow behind Mom into the living room, and for the first time, I realize that she's not always right.

Chapter Twenty

All right, my little leprechauns! It's Secret Santa time!" Mrs. Quakely calls from the back of the classroom. She's adjusting a giant foil star atop the white plastic Christmas tree. This must be the fifth time I've seen her have to retrieve it from the floor this morning. Today is the last day before Christmas break, and the entire week has been filled with Christmas carols and crafting decorations for the tree. I wish I'd been assigned the Christmas tree star. The one I made for our tree at home hasn't fallen once.

The rest of the tree is covered in shiny balls of every color, and each branch holds a tiny origami crane. The whole class made cranes. Mrs. Quakely showed us how, and we all placed our tiny birds in the tree. My crane is lavender and its beak looks more like a Labrador's snout. But I don't care. My wings are perfect.

"Leprechauns?" Mercedes howls with laughter and is quickly joined by half the class.

"I think you mean *elves*," corrects Ally.

"Elves? Yeah?" Mrs. Quakely shrugs. "Have it your way. But leprechauns have better hats!"

Secret Santa always makes my stomach flip like Olga Korbut on the uneven bars. While half of me is excited to surprise my someone with the perfect gift, chosen especially for them, the other half of me dreads the thought of their not liking what I picked out.

I don't know if Mrs. Quakely chose who each person's Secret Santa was on purpose or if it was completely random, but I ended up with, of all people, Ally! I dragged Mom across the whole mall—three blocks!—for all of Saturday trying to find the perfect gift.

"But I just don't know what she'd like," I heard myself whining, and was sure Mom was going to give me an earful about it, but instead she walked me over to the Orange Julius stand and ordered a couple of drinks for us.

"Maybe the best thing, then, is to get her something that *you*'d really love," she said. "Something *you* find special. It's always nice to introduce people you like to new things. Don't you like it when *you're* introduced to something new?"

I thought about Chaka Khan. About her voice like a lion's roar. About her hair like a lion's *mane*! I thought about her beautiful smile. Naomi introduced me to Chaka. I'll have to remember to thank her.

Mom let me pick out special wrapping paper: green with silver frosted snowflakes and a red bow for the top to make it super Christmassy. When we got home, I insisted on wrapping the present all by myself. It took me a whole hour to get it right, but in the end it was worth it.

"Nice job!" Mom said, and I could tell she was really impressed.

Mrs. Quakely fiddles behind the tree, then walks in front of it and holds up two fists full of candy canes. "Okay, leprec—I mean, *elves*, grab your presents! Once you've found your gift, come get yourself a sweet treat!"

In a flash the class is swarming the tree, sending it rocking and Christmas balls tumbling to the floor.

"Hey, hey!" calls Mrs. Quakely. "A little order, please!"

We manage to retrieve all our gifts without destroying the tree and are soon back on the rug, tearing paper and ribbons free, examining the surprises inside.

But I need to see Ally's reaction first, before I open my present. From across the room, I watch her ripping through the snowflake paper like she's killing winter. Ravaging it while Rachel stands next to her admiring her new Snoopy snow globe. Finally the paper all lies in a heap at her feet and she holds the present bare in her hands.

"A book?" barks Donald. "That's lame."

Kenny leans over his shoulder and reads the cover of Ally's gift: "*Life Goes to the Movies.*"

Ally cracks the book open and gazes at the images of stars in scenes from all sorts of films: action, drama, comedy.

"Those are *old* movies," Kenny continues. "Glad I didn't get a dumb book." He holds up his brand-new T-shirt. A bald guy in shades sucks on a lollipop next to the words:

WHO LOVES YA, BABY?

Kenny and Donald nod at the shirt approvingly.

Ally's still looking at the book, and I think she likes it. But it isn't until she turns and spots me that I realize I've been staring. She smiles and mouths the words, "Very cool."

She knows it's from me? But how?

"Open it up! Don't you wanna see what you got?" Mercedes taps the shiny red package in my hands as she runs by.

My present! I'd forgotten all about it. I take a quick look around the room to see if anyone's watching me the way I was watching Ally. If they're anxious to see my face when I open it. But no one's paying any attention to me. They're all laughing with their friends, comparing gifts, crunching candy canes.

With its shiny red paper and large gold bow that covers almost the entire thing, my gift is really pretty. And it's wrapped so neatly. I guess that rules out the class cavemen, Kenny and Donald. Thank goodness. They'd probably give me a potato bug or some rotten cheese.

I raise it to my ear and shake, but there's absolutely nothing to hear. Nothing inside moves. It's not very big. So light it could be empty. I sure hope it's not. It's only a little longer than my hand. And it's so...flat. Maybe it's a candy bar. I'll bet that's it. Candy is always a safe Secret Santa present. I mean, who doesn't like chocolate? And nobody in class really knows me or knows what I like. They probably wouldn't have any idea what to get me. I don't mind that they got me a candy bar.

I tear through the wrapping, careful not to let it all fall to the floor like most of the class did, making a mess for Mrs. Quakely to clean up later. Inside is a small package, and through the clear plastic front, I see that it's...a comb. But not a pretty one with ceramic roses or ribbons. Nothing fancy to set in my hair for special occasions. No. It's a simple plastic comb for tidying messy hair.

I take another scan of the room. Kenny and Donald are at their desks with a couple of other boys, all checking out their gifts, and I think Donald is actually trading his. Ally and Rachel are at the Christmas tree with some other kids rehanging fallen ornaments and origami cranes. Marcus and several others are gathered around Mrs. Quakely, who appears to be teaching them a dance routine. They're all too busy laughing to take notice of me or to care. And I guess whoever thought it was funny to give me a comb didn't even care enough about their stupid joke to watch for my reaction. I stare the whole class down, quietly daring my Secret Santa to reveal themselves by looking up at me. But nobody looks for my face.

Well, when they do remember their little joke and they search me out in the crowd, they're going to be disappointed. They won't find me crying in the corner or frowning like maybe they'd hoped. Instead they'll witness how strong I am and how I refuse to give in to tears.

Chapter Twenty-One

Merry Christmas, baby! Ooh, look at my pretty little niece! I could eat you up. Give me some sugar, Miss Stevie." Mona steps into the living room from outside, pulls me to her, and plants three big kisses on my cheek before stepping back and admiring the new blue velvet dress my mom has finally finished. "Look at you!" she says as she fluffs a billowy sleeve.

I look ridiculous. Like a Shirley Temple doll. Mom was supposed to have finished this dress two Christmases ago. When it didn't happen, she said, "Well, it'll make a perfect Easter dress!"

But then we passed Easter and the next Christmas came around. She still hadn't finished it. Then Easter again. Still not done. And now we're at Christmas again, and finally the dress is complete, only I've been growing all that time and, honestly, I can't believe I ever liked something so frilly. It has puffy sleeves trimmed in white lace with more lace around the neckline, and even more lace trim on the hem!

Mom's been working hard (and long!) sewing up this dress, so I'll wear it and keep my trap shut about how I really feel.

"Thank you for the Easy Bake Oven," I say. Sometimes I'd swear Aunt Mona still thinks I'm seven.

"You like it? You can practice helping your mommy in the kitchen," she says.

Aunt Mona got me a toy vacuum cleaner when I was three and has managed to find a new homemaker toy for me *every* year since.

"What'd Santa get you?" she asks.

I reach under the tree and pull out my box of Official Roller Derby roller skates. White boots with blue wheels and a blue brake, just like I wanted.

"I'd break my neck in those things. You're gonna have to show me your moves sometime!"

"I will," I promise, setting my skates back under the tree.

"Here, baby. Take this to your mommy." She deposits a glass casserole dish covered in aluminum foil in my arms and proceeds to unbutton her coat.

"Ooh. It's the marching girls!" Mona is marching in place and twirling an imaginary baton as she watches the parade on television. "Look at them. All spangled and pretty. That could be you, Stevie!"

Every inch of the kitchen counter is covered in bowls of cooked vegetables, uncooked vegetables, dishes covered in foil, utensils, seasonings. Pots bubble on the stove, their savory goodness filling the room. Even with all that food, Naomi is chopping something on a cutting board.

"Mona here?" asks Mom. She's bent over fussing with something in the oven.

"Yeah. She brought this." I part a space between dishes and set down the casserole.

"She needs to get in here!" Mom calls down the hall, "Mona!"

Mona quickly appears.

"I'm here. I'm here. Calm yourself, Kitty cat," she says, and lays a kiss on my mom's cheek.

"Here." Mom thrusts a large spoon into Mona's hand and goes to the oven. She removes a big brown bird from inside.

"You gonna make me work?" Mona says, laughing, and crosses to Naomi. She plants a fat kiss on her cheek before going to the turkey and getting to her job of basting.

"Kitty, you should get Stevie into a parade. She could be one of those marching girls!"

"Majorettes," corrects Mom.

Mona ladles a last spoonful of brown juice over the bird, tosses the spoon into the sink, and goes to the fridge. "I want some eggnog!" She searches a beat before pulling the carton out, then hits the cupboard in search of a glass.

"Here we go!" She retrieves four glasses. "Who's joining me? Who wants some eggnog?"

"I do!" I say.

"Me too!" says Naomi.

"Okay, Stevie, here's yours." She hands me a small glass of pale yellow nog. "Here you go, Nay Nay. And here's mine. But it's gonna need a little something more...." She's back to the cupboards. Even I know she's searching for whiskey this time.

"Up there." Mom points an elbow to the cupboard above the refrigerator without skipping a beat as she mashes potatoes.

Mona grins and dances her way to the cupboard. "Here I come. Here I come...."

Mom shakes her head. "You're silly."

"Yes," she sings, stretching to reach the bottle. "Yes I am." Mona lets out a hearty laugh and looks at me, eyes wide, as she tops off her nog.

I let out a laugh and Mom gives me a smirk. I know she thinks my laughing only "encourages" Mona to act crazier, but I can't help it. She's funny. And *fun*. She knows how to bring the party wherever she goes, and it's nice to have someone jolly in the house.

Mona reaches over and twists a curl at the nape of Mom's neck.

"You know that sweet girl Monica, down the hall from me? She does hair and she could smooth your hair out and bump some pretty waves into it."

Mom gently swats Mona's fingers away.

"I'm enjoying my natural," she says. "It's a little more effort than it looks like, but then, I was shoving it all under a wig, so I guess anything's going to be a little more effort than that."

"I love your hair, Aunt Kitty! It'll get easier. You'll see," says Naomi. "I sure don't miss getting my hair hot-ironed. All that fuss. I'm done! I love my natural."

"But Nay Nay, your hair was so pretty," whines Mona.

"And my natural is *fierce*!" she says, and bounds out of the room, clearly done with the conversation.

Mona turns to Mom and squinches up her nose.

"Her hair needed a break from all those chemicals and heat anyway, Mona." She runs a hand over Mona's flattened hair, pulled back in a tight bun. "Yours could use a break, too, you know?"

Mona pulls back. "Don't you start trying to convert me. Make me all crazy hippie child like the two of you. No, no, no." She waves her hands over her head. "I like my smooth tresses," she says, and smiles a big, silly grin at me.

My dad enters from the hall.

"Uh-oh. Trouble! Who ordered a side of trouble?" he teases as he passes Mona, quickly ducking and shielding his head from her blows.

"You better get moving!" she says. "Or give me a kiss. Come on, Coop. Give your big sis a smooch!" She goes after him and tries to corner him as he pretends to scream, but he's soon saved by the doorbell.

"Oh, Stevie, can you get that?" asks Mom. "It's your uncle Owen." I start for the front door but am quickly cut off by Mona.

"Owen?" She takes her nog *and* my mom's and swishes out of the kitchen. "You stay here, Lil' Stevie Wonder. I'll get the door. Nobody told me my boyfriend was coming to the party!"

Later, Burl Ives wishes us a "Holly Jolly Christmas" from the living room record player as we all sit around the dinner table in the kitchen.

"You all feel that earthquake the other day?" Owen asks.

"There was an earthquake?" Naomi asks. She sits up, face full of worry.

"Not a biggie: 3.5, I think," says Owen.

"Paper said 3.7," Dad corrects. "I didn't feel a thing. You?"

Owen chuckles and says, "Well, I'll tell you, in that tin can of mine it doesn't take more than a garbage truck rolling by to give you a good shake. I may have felt it but thought it was a cat jumping on the roof." Then he turns to Naomi. "Don't you worry. Every time we have a little one, it takes more pressure off that big one we're due for," he says before diving back into his ear of corn. His style of eating corn is a little like the cartoons: part wild boar, part electric typewriter. I think he's on a mission to finish this ear quickly so he can eat another. Living in his van, Owen doesn't get a good home-cooked meal often. He doesn't even have a kitchen! Mom's always asking him to join us for supper, but he's always making excuses as to why he can't. He's afraid he'll be too much trouble. But he can't turn down holidays. It's nice to see him at our table enjoying all this food instead of in his van eating beans from a can.

Mona turns to Owen. "You got a healthy appetite. Don't ya, Owen?"

"What's that?" Owen looks up from his corn, a yellow kernel teetering on his lip.

"I said you got a healthy appetite. Ain't that right?" She smiles at him and winks.

"All right, Mona, eat your food. C'mon," says my dad, chuckling a little, but I can tell he really does hope she'll stop.

Owen's ears have gone fuchsia.

"Oh, I'm sorry. Am I eating like a pig?" he asks with all sincerity.

"No, no!" Mom assures him, then cuts Mona a look that says *enough*.

Mona laughs. "Nope. Don't take it like that, O. Not what I meant at all." She gets up and starts opening kitchen cabinets, leaving her shoes somewhere under the table. "I need me some more nog.... But where did nog's friend go?"

Dad whispers to my mom, "I hope you hid that whiskey."

Naomi turns to me. "I wanna see you on your new skates. They're so cool!"

"I know!" I say. "Can we go to the park?"

"I'm too stuffed now, but maybe tomorrow," she says, unbuttoning the top button of her jeans. "Mona, you ever seen Stevie skate? Girl is so good!"

"Ooh! Maybe you could be a figure skater," Mona says, eyes wide.

"Or a Roller Derby queen," says Naomi, bumping me with her forearms.

Dad groans.

"Oh, that's right," says Naomi, and then she switches to a low voice, a fake "man's" voice. "Women shouldn't play sports. Those women that do are just trying to be men!"

"Oh please. That's not what I said. And let's not start up with that women's lib nonsense again," Dad says. He lets out a short, dry laugh. He clearly doesn't want to talk about this, but it looks like Naomi's just getting started.

"*Nonsense?* You don't think that women should be treated equally, Uncle Coop? Are you gonna tell me that you don't think that your wife, your *daughter*, should be given the same respect as men? That if Aunt Kitty was working the same job as a man that she shouldn't be given equal pay?"

"Well, Kitty will never have to work because I—the man—make sure of that," he says. "I provide for my family. That's my job."

"Yes, brother Coop!" Mona says, raising her glass and throwing Dad a big smile.

"What?" Naomi says. She shakes her head, laughing. "Uncle Coop! I can't believe you. I thought a man like you would be down with the women's movement. You married a sister! I thought you'd be down with empowering *all* oppressed people. But you are a bona fide *chauvinist*!"

"I don't know what that's supposed to mean," he says. "I don't care about any 'movement.' I didn't marry Kitty to make some point. I married your aunt because I love her."

"Amen to love!" Mona says, trying to keep things light. "Can I get an amen, Owen?"

"Oh. Uh, sure," he says, raising his water glass to clink with her eggnog.

"Kitty, why don't you bring the pies out? Let's get to dessert." Dad motions to Mom in the kitchen. His neck is getting red and I'm pretty sure he wants to change the subject.

Mom comes through and grabs a couple of plates. "Give me a hand, Stevie," she says.

"Wait a minute. Why don't you help clear, Uncle Coop? What? Is that only a woman's job?" Naomi's voice is a little loud. She was teasing before, but now? Now I'm not so sure.

"Hey now, Naomi," Mom says. "That's enough."

Mona chimes in, "Girl, you'd better show some respect in this man's house."

Naomi looks away and sucks her teeth.

Dad chuckles. But it's not a happy chuckle. "I hope you're not this rude to your boyfriend," he says.

Naomi's jaw tightens.

"You got yourself a boyfriend out here already?" asks Mona. From the kitchen counter, Mom whips around to look at Naomi, waiting for her answer.

Naomi shoots a look at me. A look that clearly wants to know if I told. I give her my very best I-have-no-idea-what-he's-talking-about eyes without drawing any attention. And it's the truth. I haven't told a soul about Jimmy.

"No!" Naomi says. She lets out a short laugh as she hands me her empty plate. "He's crazy."

"Am I?" asks Dad, turning to Naomi and grinning. Taunting.

And suddenly I realize that he's not just teasing. He *knows*! He must've heard some of her phone calls. I haven't been thinking about erasing Naomi's calls. Maybe I should have. But then there's that booby trap. I haven't heard Mom on any strange calls since I discovered it, but if I do, I'm ever-so-carefully sliding under that thing and grabbing the recorder.

"Okay, okay. Enough, you two," Mom says, turning to the table with an apple pie in one hand and a sweet potato pie in the other. "Naomi—be nice to your uncle. And Coop, just leave her alone."

"Is it okay if I go to Sandra's now?" Naomi asks. She's still mad at my dad, I can tell.

"You're gonna try to eat a *second* meal?" Mom asks. I try not to look at Naomi. I'm afraid she'll be able to tell that *I* know it's really Jimmy she's going to see.

"No," Naomi says. She looks at my mom when she speaks, but her voice is higher than usual. "I just promised I'd stop by, is all."

As Naomi crosses out of the kitchen, my dad smiles at her. "You kids have fun."

It's not Christmas until I've watched *It's a Wonderful Life*. It might be my very favorite old movie. And ever since Mom and I stopped watching our Friday Night Movies I haven't really watched *any* old movies lately. But I've seen this one so many times that I practically know it by heart, which is a good thing since I'm only half watching the TV. Mostly I'm being entertained by Mona.

She's back to flirting. Bent over the record player, flipping through the albums, directly—and quite intentionally—blocking Uncle Owen's view of the television. Her butt shifts from left to right as she studies the records.

"Y'all gonna put me to sleep with this boring show!" Mona whines, and lets out a wide-mouthed yawn. "We should put some more music on. More fun than watching that stupid program. Don't you think so, Owen?" she asks without turning.

"Uh, either way is fine with me," he stammers as he stands and heads for the hall bathroom.

"Don't you all have any more records? Shoot! You only got like five!"

I remember the Chaka Khan album under my mattress. "I'll be right back!" I say, and dash upstairs. This is perfect. I can listen to the album and then finally return it to Naomi's stack.

I quickly return, shake the album free, and hand the cover to Mona.

"She's really good," I say. But before I can set it on the player, Mona protests.

"Uh-uh! No thank you. I do not need to hear this wild child!" She's staring at the photo of Chaka on the back of the album cover. "Is she even wearing a bra? Look at her, looking all crazy." She lets out a loud yawn, tosses the cover onto the couch, and walks off down the hall.

I grab the album cover and look at Chaka. I think it's Mona who's crazy. Chaka's beautiful.

"I'm leaving!" Mona announces loudly as she enters the kitchen. I can hear her saying her goodbyes to my mom and dad. And then there's a ruckus. Laughing and shouting.

My dad comes running from the kitchen, laughing and covering his head. Mona's quick on his heels.

"You'd better let me kiss you goodbye, boy!" They wrestle a moment until he manages to free himself and take off upstairs.

"Merry Christmas to you, too!" she yells after him, then grabs her coat from the couch. "Bye, baby girl." She blows me a kiss.

As Uncle Owen walks out of the bathroom, Mona calls to him. "Walk me to my car, Owen."

As soon as they're out the door, I run upstairs and put Naomi's album back in her room. I'll wait for one of our hangouts to finally listen to it.

On the street below, I can hear Mona and Uncle Owen.

She stumbles up to his van grinning, asks if he really lives in there.

"Yes, ma'am, I do."

"Where you take a bath?"

I never thought about that before. Where *does* he take a bath?

She laughs and walks unevenly across the street to her brown Lincoln Continental. After several failed attempts to open the car door, Owen gently takes the keys from her and directs her to his van.

"Let me give you a ride, Mona."

"Ooh! I get to see the mystery van!" she howls as he helps her climb into the passenger seat. "Thank you, Santa Claus!"

I watch the big white van disappear into the night; I can hear whispers of Christmas carols in the distance.

Back in my room, I unzip and let the pile of velvet and lace pool around my ankles. I throw on jeans and a T-shirt, unbraid my hair, and shake it free. Ahh. No longer a doll. On my way out of my room, I catch my reflection in the mirror and I have to stop.

It's unmistakable, but as I look at myself there in my T-shirt and jeans, with my hair let loose, I see the girl from the album. I see Chaka. And I can't help but smile.

Chapter Twenty-Two

I'm still on Christmas break when Mom pops her head in my room.

"Hey, pumpkin. Your dad and I are going to dinner."

Whoa. Dinner together? Does that mean everything's okay with them? Does that mean Clarence is no longer in the picture?

"Really? Like on a *date*?" I ask.

She laughs. "I guess you could call it that."

The phone rings and she jogs to her room to grab it.

"Hello?... Oh, hi.... You did? That's great." She closes the bedroom door behind her.

Between the closed door and the hushed tone of her voice, it's clear Clarence is very much still in the picture.

I'm about to run to my clubhouse but have another idea.

I zip toward Naomi's room, where she's set the blue phone just outside her door. Careful to press my finger on the receiver as I lift the phone from the hook, I put it to my ear and then gently release my finger so that my mom and whoever else is on the line won't hear me listening in.

"I can't come tonight. Coop and I are going to dinner. I couldn't get out of it," says Mom.

Naomi's doorknob turns and I quickly hang up the phone as quietly as possible. I pretend I'm taking it down the hall.

"You going to be on long?" Naomi asks. "I need to make a call."

"Oh...no, I won't," I say.

She nods and disappears into the bathroom.

While I didn't have a chance to hear much, I'm still sure Mom was talking to Clarence.

Downstairs, the front door opens and my dad calls out, "Hello!" to whoever can hear him. I run downstairs. He's standing there in his sharp creased trousers and white shirt, fussing with newspapers and his briefcase. When he sees me come running, he laughs.

"Heya, kiddo." I throw my arms around him. "What's with you?"

"Nothing. Just happy to see you. How was your day?" I ask, following him to the kitchen.

"Pretty good," he says, dipping a large spoon into a pot of sloppy joe meat and shoving a mouthful into his face. "Yours?"

I nod. "Good, good."

"Everything okay? You seem kind of twitchy," he says. And he's right. I can hear my heart beating in my chest and I can't stand still. I've got to get downstairs and erase that call before Dad hears it.

"Me? I'm fine," I say.

"Your mom and I are going to dinner," he says, pulling apart a dinner roll. "I'm starving. Can you do me a favor and see how far off she is?"

When I get upstairs, Naomi is in Mom's doorway. "So, you think you'll be back before midnight?" I peek over Naomi's shoulder and watch Mom ready herself for the night out. She dabs polka dots of creamy concealer under each eye, then slides a streak straight down the middle of her nose. She turns to answer Naomi, but seeing me there, she strikes a wild animal pose and growls.

"Grrr." She doesn't look like a beast as much as a friendly Disney cheetah. One that I don't particularly feel like laughing or playing with right now.

Mom turns to Naomi. "We might. Could be earlier. But Naomi—no company while we're gone." She inspects her edges to be sure every hair is tucked neatly under her Ava wig. I haven't seen her wear one of her wigs in weeks now. Maybe she really is trying to make things better with Dad.

"I know, I know." Naomi rolls her eyes and turns down the hall.

"Dad wants to know how long you'll be," I say.

"Be ready in ten," she says, swiping a kiss of raspberry across her lips.

I tell Dad, then go back to my room, flop down on my bed, and stare up at the cottage cheese ceiling. As soon as they're gone, I'm going to listen to the rest of that call and erase it.

But after that, maybe I should just tell Mom about the recorder. Sure, she'll be mad at first, but I don't know how long I can keep this up. Trying to hide her secret. And while I know she won't like my being "nosy," I think it's also time I tell her that I know about Clarence and that I want her to stop seeing him.

Mom appears at my door.

"So, we're about to head out, pumpkin. We won't be gone too long. But don't wait up, okay?"

"Okay."

"I love you."

"Good night."

Mom goes to Naomi's room, rattles off the name of a

restaurant and when she thinks they'll be home, and is soon downstairs and at the front door with my dad.

I'm on my way to Naomi's room. I'm thinking just maybe she'll watch a movie with me, but the baby-blue cord disappears under her door, and I can hear her already on the phone. I lean against her door and listen.

"I'll get there early and set up. Just tell Jackie to bring extra chairs."

Sounds like some school stuff so I'd better not interrupt the call.

Fine. Looks like another solo Stevie movie night.

As I near the bottom of the stairs I see that Mom has already gone out to the car and my dad is straggling behind. His hair is neatly coiffed, shoes shined, suit jacket draped over his arm. But with his free hand, he bangs at a couple patches of pale dust on the knees of his trousers.

When did he get all dirty?

I stop short and back up a couple stairs so he can't see me.

He fusses with the jacket over his arm. Pulling it and adjusting it. Is he hiding something under there?

He checks that his trousers are clean in front once more, then smooths his hair in the mirror, and leaves.

As soon as he's out the door, I dash through the living room, through the kitchen, and out back. I throw the door of my hideout open and aim the flashlight behind the water heater. The spoons lie in the powdery gray on the floor. Behind them, there's nothing. Just a faint rectangular outline of where the recorder used to be.

Oh no.

Dad must've listened to the tape, to that last conversation Mom had with Clarence. Does he plan on surprising her with it? Playing the recording for her to prove that he knows what she's been up to?

I run out the side gate to the street. I have to tell Mom. I should've told her before. But as I reach the front of our building, they've already pulled off and away. Are rounding the corner. A red turn light winks and they're gone.

How will he do it? What will he say? What will *she* say?

My mind starts whizzing through all the old movies I've ever watched.

I can just imagine. . . .

They turn off Lincoln Boulevard and onto the freeway like they always do, but then Dad makes a sudden, unfamiliar turn, getting off at a strange exit.

"What're you doing?" she asks.

"Shortcut," he says.

She looks outside and realizes she's on a street she doesn't recognize.

"Coop, where are you taking us?"

"You think I'm stupid?" he says, eyes still on the road, shaking his head.

"What are you talking about? Where are we going?"

The streets are empty now. Not a person in sight.

"I'm onto you, Kitty. I knew you were up to no good!"

"That's enough, Coop. What's going on?" she shouts.

Finally he turns onto a dirt road and stops the car. He sets the cassette player on the seat between them. But she still doesn't understand. Not until he presses play.

Through the crackle, she hears Clarence's voice followed by her own. Then the two of them laughing together. Laughing at him.

"It's not what you think," she stammers.

"You can't fool me, Kitty," he says. "I want a divorce."

That's it. That's got to be what he has planned. I need to reach her. To let her know that he has that tape. That he knows her secret.

I turn to run up the stairs, to tell Naomi. Maybe she can call the restaurant before he plays the tape. Give her a chance to tell him on her own.

I'm moving so fast that as I approach the top step, I don't see Elvis. I don't even realize he's there until my body is lurching forward, feet tangled round his middle, and with full force my head strikes the wall and I go down.

My parents used to pick me up and carry me to bed whenever I'd fall asleep in front of the TV. In my half sleep, it felt good to be carried. Bundled in a blanket and nestled in their arms, I always felt safe.

It rarely happens anymore. Mom says I'm too big, too long, too heavy.

"You want me to break my back?"

But tonight Naomi put me in bed.

I vaguely remember her kneeling next to me on the hall carpet.

"Stevie? Stevie! You okay?"

My hand goes to the tender lump on my head as it starts to come back to me.

"I heard that boom from all the way down the hall."

She lifted me up onto my feet and led me to my room. I climbed into bed. She gave me water and a bag of frozen peas for my head. Read something to me.

"And the bagpipe said, 'Aoogga!' "

We both laughed.

And then I must have fallen asleep.

But now I'm in Mom's arms. She's lifted me from my bed.... Where is she taking me? Downstairs? I begin to come to a little. Just enough to crack open my eyes. The living room is dark; the only light is that of the kitchen's filtering in gently down the hall. And then I see...Is that Dad? Yes. It's his silhouette in the hall. He's just standing there. I can barely make out his face. It's too dark. But he doesn't say a thing, or even move. He just watches us as we disappear out the front door.

The air is cool on me now. We're outside. And Mom's feet are moving fast. Even lugging my sleepy dead weight, she daintily trots across our walkway like a deer crossing a highway. Her breath is quick and shallow.

I force my eyes open.

"Mom—" I start, but she quickly shushes me and opens the car door. Our Pinto blends into the night. Its metallic finish sparkles like the stars. She deposits me into the back and the door closes behind me like a vault. When I sit up straight, my head throbs.

Mom moves silently around the back of the car, and she's mumbling to herself as she gets in. It isn't until she's closed the door behind her that I realize there's someone already sitting in the front. Sloped deep in the passenger seat is Naomi. She turns to me and whispers.

"How's your head?"

With the tips of my fingers grazing the lump, I nod. "Okay." Though I'm not sure I really am. "What's happening?"

But Naomi just turns back to face forward.

"C'mon, Kitty. Come on." Mom's struggling to find the key to the ignition among a ring full of them. She drops the whole thing on the car floor. "Damnit," she loudly whispers. She sits up and finally locates the key, fires the car up. Thunder against a still, silent night. No one is out. The windows of the apartments across the street are dark. Everyone's asleep. A streetlamp bathes us in a halo of white.

"Did something bad happen tonight, Aunt Kitty? I mean, why're we just leaving like this?" Her voice trails off a bit as she looks out the passenger window.

"No, no. It's just..." Mom stops for a moment, takes a deep breath, and stares down our walkway. Is she waiting for Dad to come out? "It was...just time. I just needed to go."

Time? Time for what?

I'm watching the walkway now, too. I don't know where we're going in the middle of the night, but...is Dad coming with us? And if he's not...

"Poor Uncle Coop," Naomi says, burying her face in her hands.

Mom shakes her head and I think she's about to explain. To tell us where we're going, what's going on, but all she says is "It was time."

We drive through the black streets in silence before

finally arriving at Sandra's corner. Mom throws the car in park.

"You sure you're good here?" Mom asks Naomi.

"I'm okay." Naomi looks at me in the back. "See you later, cuz."

"Tell Sandra's mom thank you. Give her that number." Mom motions at a square of paper in Naomi's hand. Naomi holds it up and nods at Mom. Gives her a shaky smile and Mom forces one back.

We've rolled along for blocks before Mom finally speaks.

"I know this all seems strange, Stevie." She finally turns to me. "But maybe we can look at it like an adventure!" She's nodding and trying to smile. I don't say anything. I can't smile or nod.

Mom goes back to looking straight ahead, staring into the night as it streams past.

I lie down on the back seat and search the sky beyond the window. A blanket of black. Red and green lights dot the intersections that stop us.

The air seeping in from the passenger window is getting cooler and I smell the ocean. I bet Clarence lives in Malibu. With that big ol' Cadillac, he probably lives right on the sand.

We go over a small bump, the car slows, then stops, and I hear the parking brake engage. I sit up just as Mom cuts the engine.

I have no idea where we are. But then it is dark and it's really late. There isn't a single person outside.

A blazing yellow arrow flickers off and on, pointing to the entrance of an orange-and-brown hotel. A cartoon tiger peeks from behind it. A weak bulb in its friendly eye causes it to wink rapidly.

Once in the lobby, Mom goes to the front desk and talks to a man with a single fat eyebrow that shades his eyes like a patio awning. I swear he's as small as a fifth grader and it looks like his neck is floating in his wide shirt collar.

While Mom deals with that guy, I search the lobby for Clarence. I bet he'll be meeting us here any minute. But he's the last person I want to see right now. With his "I'm your best friend" smile and his Creature from the Black Lagoon voice. He'd better steer clear of me.

An adventure. How can Mom think *any* of this can be an adventure?

The display stand beside me offers all sorts of *real* adventures. Skydiving, helicopter rides, Six Flags Magic Mountain Amusement Park. Maybe our "adventure" will finally take me to Disneyland.

Mom walks back to me holding a key attached to an orange plastic tiger. After a short elevator ride and a walk down the long, carpeted halls, we arrive at our room.

I stare into the tidy space. Still no Clarence.

"Go on in, pumpkin," Mom says.

I step inside and drag my fingers across the polyester bedcover. A painting of the sea hangs on the wall behind the beds. A huge bird hovers over a crashing wave that's flung a fish into the sky. At the far end of the room, parted orange drapes reveal a sliver of moon high above the real Pacific Ocean. A sliding glass door leads to a balcony and outside the palm trees sway. I can't see the water, but I can hear the waves.

"You can play in the pool tomorrow," Mom says, tapping the suitcase she's hoisted atop one of the beds. "I brought your swimsuit."

Mom's sitting on the bed. Sunken face. She looks exhausted, but I wish she would speak.

"Mom, what's going on?" I ask.

She shakes her head and pats the space next to her. When I go to her, she pushes my hair behind my ear, grazing the new bump there, as she fluffs the top and sides.

"Don't," I say, pulling away. "Tell me."

"Listen, sweetheart, your daddy and I...we aren't happy." Her eyes immediately well up and she drops her chin. When she continues talking, I can hear the tremble in her voice. "I think you know that. We can't seem to see eye to eye, and...we're going to have to spend some time apart for a while."

My stomach feels tight.

"Are we moving out?"

She takes a deep breath, then looks up at me and nods. "Maybe...I'm not sure completely. We'll see. We'll see." Then she quickly adds, "But you'll still go to the same school. You won't be leaving your friends."

I can't help but let out a dry laugh. *What friends?* That's the least of my worries. "What about Naomi?"

"We'll go get her from Sandra's in the morning," she says. "I wanted us to have some time to ourselves."

"Does she know you guys are..." She didn't say *divorce*. She said *time apart*. I know what they call that. "Separating?"

"No," she says, shaking her head and looking down again. She pushes at her cuticles and twists her wedding ring around and around. "I haven't had a chance yet to..." Her voice trails off.

I don't know if she's ever going to come clean with the truth. But I can't wait any longer so I say it for her.

"Are we going to move in with your boyfriend?"

She darts her head up and wipes her eyes. "What?"

I don't flinch. I summon all my Cleopatra Jones bravery.

"Clarence," I say. "I know he's your boyfriend. Naomi knows, too. And now, I guess Dad does, right?"

Mom opens her mouth to speak, but nothing comes out. She reaches down and pulls off one shoe and then the other. Rests them side by side near the wall. Slowly, she approaches the desk, leans against it, and just stares at me. I stare back. I don't back down, even though I'm beginning to feel like I'm definitely in trouble.

"That's quite an accusation, Stevie. What makes you say that?"

"Well, you're always with him and going to the library, staying out late with him, and...talking to him on the phone."

I'm trying to be brave but am beginning to feel *my* voice tremble.

"What?" The anger in Mom's voice is clear now, and I start to feel even worse. "How do you know that? Did your father tell you that?"

"No! I heard you on the phone with him! You said you couldn't tell Dad about the two of you because he'd put a stop to it. I heard you!" It comes out angrier than I realized I was. "I know it was wrong of Dad to tap the phone—"

"Wait, you *knew* your dad was tapping our phone?"

"But he must've done it because he knew you had a boyfriend! I mean, I know. I saw—"

"You saw? You saw *what*, Stevie? You saw *what*?"

Mom could burn a clean hole in me with that glare. I

suddenly don't feel as sure. What did I see? I saw her that time in the library talking to him and laughing. He gave us a ride in his big car and they were all smiling. He called the house. She's spent so much *time* with him! What else could it be?

Mom watches me twitch and stammer for a minute, unable to confidently answer her, and then she softens and sighs. "Oh, Stevie!" She shakes her head. Puts her face in her hands. "You don't know anything, Stevie!" She looks back up at me and her face is so sad. "Pumpkin, I went back to school. I went back to school! I've been taking college classes at night. I'm working on getting my degree in library science. To be a librarian. Clarence is taking the same course, and he helped me with books, but other than that he's just been a good friend. And I've needed a friend these last few months."

Some phantom has grabbed hold of my throat with one hand and my stomach with the other and is slowly squeezing them. I can barely swallow. My arms feel cold, but my face is so hot.

"But you told Clarence on the phone that..." I sputter.

Mom nods. "Your dad didn't know. Couldn't know. He wouldn't have let me go. You've heard him shout it enough times, sweetheart."

My brain is slowly catching up with what she's telling

me. The extra visits to the library without me. The late nights. Clarence calling the house. It's all making sense.

"But why didn't you just tell me?" My shoulders are shaking and I can hardly see through the wall of tears about to fall.

"Oh, Stevie." Mom pulls me to her and, rocking me from side to side, speaks into my hair. "Like I said, your dad didn't know. I didn't want *you* to have to lie."

If only she knew how good I am at it.

Over late-night burgers and fries from room service, Mom tells me all about school. *Her* school sounds so much different from mine. There are no cliquey groups. No eating alone in the cafeteria. No bullies or mean girls. Mom *loves* school. Her professor has them reading books from all over the world. They discuss the stories, and through the discussions she says she discovers all sorts of things she wouldn't have uncovered on her own. There's a lot of reading and she's been spending a lot of time at the library writing papers, but she says that even though it's hard, it brings her so much joy.

"That sounds so cool. I want to go to college one day," I say.

"You will." Mom smiles. A real smile.

We slide into starched sheets and Mom cuddles me close. The balcony door is still open and I can hear the sea.

My brain, my legs, my fingernails are all limp with exhaustion. But I feel safe tonight. Here, just me, Mom, and the truth. Everything is kind of okay again. Her quiet snoring mingles with the whisper of the ocean waves and their gentle song lulls me to sleep.

Chapter Twenty-Three

In the morning, Mom is up before me.

I crack one eye open and scope out my strange sur-
roundings. The bright shard of light from the balcony cutting the room in half, the stinging smell of bleach mingled
with stale burgers and ketchup. There's brown paisley
everywhere. On the bed, on the drapes.

"Stevie?" Mom reaches down and brushes the back of
her hand across my cheek. She looks rested today. She's
ditched the Ava and her afro looks freshly combed. "Why
don't you run down to the pool now so you can have plenty
of time? I'm going to check us out and then give Sandra's
mom a call."

As I sit up, I feel the lump on my head and am happy
to find it's almost completely gone. Just feels bruised now.

Memories of last night, of where I am and all that happened, come rushing in. How I told Mom that I knew about her "boyfriend." That *Clarence* was her boyfriend. Her confusion and surprise.

I think about Dad's watching us go from the shadows.

Are we really leaving my dad for a while? Forever? Where will we go? Can you live in a hotel?

"No running!" An elderly woman with orange-peel skin and a floppy hat is sunbathing as she shouts at me on my way to the stairs that lead into the pool. I take it she thinks she's the pool police.

I climb in, slowly at first, and then lunge forward and all the way under, flattening my palms on the pool's floor, straightening my body so my toes reach for the sky. A perfect handstand. I practice my handstands for a while, timing myself to see how long I can stay up, perfectly straight, without toppling. I'm good at handstands. I used to be better than the rest of the Polliwogs, including Jennifer... when she was a Polliwog.

I read the numbers along the edges of the pool that signify how deep the water is in feet: 3, 5, 8.

I'm standing in 3. I walk closer to the number 5 and begin to feel the water rise a little higher on my chest. I go to the edge and, holding on to the warm, round border, scoot closer and closer to the five. Soon, the water is past my chest. It's at my shoulders, then covers them entirely, and I realize I'm holding my chin up, trying to keep it from dipping into the pool. To go any farther, I need to tiptoe. Finally I am on my tippy-toes, chin raised, water on my neck, still clutching the rim. If I could just push off the wall. Just swim across the middle.

Do it, Stevie.

But as I hesitate, I realize that my fingers are holding on so tightly to the edge of the pool they may have to call the paramedics to pry them free. I just can't do it. I'm too chicken. Besides, if I started to sink, the lady in the hat wouldn't help me. She'd probably just scold me for drowning.

When we pick Naomi up from Sandra's, the first thing she does is reach across the gear shift to Mom in the driver's seat and hold her tight. She doesn't even say anything. She just gives her a big old hug, that I quickly see from Mom's face, eyes closed and smiling, she needed.

"Thank you, Naomi," she says, still glued to my cousin's shoulder.

When they finally separate, Naomi asks Mom, "You okay?"

Mom nods, still smiling. "I am."

Naomi turns to me in the back seat. "How about you, cuz?"

I give her a thumbs-up. "There was a pool at the hotel," I say.

"That's cool," she says.

"Yeah, I wish you could've come," I say.

"I'll bet it was fun," she says, but her attention is back on my mom. Naomi seems to be checking her for cracks. "Have you spoken with Uncle Coop since..."

Mom takes a deep breath and finishes making her left turn before she says, "Yes, Naomi, I have."

"While I was in the pool?" I interrupt.

"Uh-huh."

We turn onto our street and I search for Dad's car. "Is Dad here?" I don't know what to say to him if he *is* home. I've never seen him as sad as he seemed last night.

"No, sweetheart. I want to talk to you both about everything."

We sit in the kitchen drinking Kool-Aid and Mom tells us that Dad has agreed to move out. That it may just be temporary, but he's already left.

"Already? When? Where'd he go?"

Without even meaning to, I'm turning my head toward the living room, then looking out back through the patio's glass door. Searching. I look up to my parents' room and listen. But what am I listening for? What am I looking for? It's as if some part of me doesn't believe her. Like I think

248

my dad's going to magically appear or that I'll hear him in another room and that, I don't know, that everything will be back to normal, I guess. That none of this would have happened.

"Listen, pumpkin," she says. "Your dad and I talked last night after you went to sleep and we talked for quite a bit today. You're going to see him all the time. We just can't be together right now. And...maybe not ever." She gently pulls my hand from my mouth so I'll stop chewing my nails and says, "But it's all going to be okay. I promise."

She tells Naomi all about how she went back to school and how she's sorry she kept it secret. I'm thinking maybe Naomi needs to come clean about *her* secret, but I know *that's* not gonna happen. As Mom talks and explains and apologizes, her eyes keep watering up and she wipes the tears away with the back of her hand before they can fall.

"Coop and I are actually going to meet and talk in a little bit. Hash things out," she says.

"I'm so proud of you, Aunt Kitty," Naomi says.

"Well, I don't know if it's something to be..." Mom takes a deep breath. "But...thank you, Naomi. It's kind of scary."

Naomi nods at her, smiling, and no one says anything for a minute. There's a big fat awkward silence sitting on the table in front of us. Naomi finally speaks.

"What's he going to do?" she asks, and now I can see *her* eyes welling up with tears.

My mom turns back to the table. To the big silence. Sadness hangs heavy over her face.

I feel so helpless. There's nothing I can do to change this. It's happened. I can't imagine life without my dad around, even if I do still get to see him a lot. That's not the same.

I remember what Aunt Flo said. "Some folks get stuck in their ways. Just not used to change." She was talking about Dad's sisters, but I guess it's true about Dad, too. Mom has changed. And maybe, even though *she's* happier, he's still stuck.

Chapter Twenty-Four

Hurry up, Stevie. Your dad will be here in five minutes."

Dad's taking me to dinner. Italian. We've talked on the phone a lot since he moved out a couple of months ago, but tonight will be the first time we've *seen* each other.

"Why don't you wear that pretty velvet dress your mommy made?" Mona says, eyeing my outfit. She's clearly not having my smock top and plaid pants.

"She doesn't have time to change," Mom says. "He's going to honk and you'll go out, grab the mail for him, and meet him out there." She turns to Mona and says pointedly, "He's not coming in."

"Don't look at me!" Mona holds up her hands. "I wasn't gonna say nothing you wouldn't want me to say." Under her breath she continues, "Can't for the life of me understand why someone would leave a good man. But that's just me."

Mom rolls her eyes and puts a plate of Hamburger Helper and peas in front of Mona before serving herself.

Naomi enters the kitchen and gives Aunt Mona a kiss. "Hiya, Auntie." She looks over my outfit on her way to get a plate from the cupboard. "You look fancy. Tonight when you see your dad?"

"Yeah. He's taking me out for Italian food," I say.

Naomi loads up her plate and takes a seat across from Mona. "Nice!"

"I know!"

It's strange but, as excited as I am to see him, I'm also a little nervous. I think it's because I don't ever do things with *just* my dad. Mom is always there. Dinners out have always been all three of us together. I guess, like Mrs. Quakely would say, I'm entering a new chapter of my life.

"Ooh! Aunt Kitty," Naomi starts. "I keep meaning to ask you. There's a big community service and food give-away next week. I wanna go volunteer and I was hoping you could drive me. It's all the way in East LA."

"Well, let me know when," says Mom. "You and Sandra doing that together?"

Naomi hesitates and I know that pause means Jimmy is somehow involved. "She might.... She might...."

"Your mom will be pleased to hear you're helping the community," says Mom.

"Yeah, it's really cool, and..." Another hesitation. "I was thinking that you might wanna check it out, Aunt Kitty. They're some really together people doing what they can to help those who need it. Feeding folks, educating them..."

Naomi ignores me when she sees my eyes widen in shock. Is she really going to introduce Mom to Jimmy?

"Look at my niece! Helping those less fortunate!" says Mona. "You need to come to church with me. They could use your help serving at the Church Dinner Thursdays."

"I've been helping once a week with their breakfast program for kids," Naomi continues.

"Naomi, that's great!" says Mom.

"I'm always trying to tell my mom all the good that the Panther Party does, but she just thinks—"

"Panther Party?" Mona says more like a hiss, and shakes her head. "Those folks with the automatic weapons? Bunch of rabblerousers."

"What's a babblerusser?" I ask.

"*Rabblerouser!*" Mona repeats.

"They're troublemakers," Mom says, frowning. "And I didn't realize it was the Panthers you were getting involved with, Naomi."

"What? They aren't troublemakers," Naomi says. "They're only trying to—"

Mona turns to my mom. "Kitty, they scare me."

"And me. The whole idea when you came west, Naomi, was to get away from bad influences," says Mom.

"You all are listening to that news propaganda," Naomi says.

"Those guns aren't propaganda. I can see that with my own eyes," says Mom. "No, Naomi. I'm sorry."

"But if you could just see the good they're—"

"Naomi, you can do better," says Mona, slathering butter on a dinner roll. "Now that's enough. Your auntie has spoken." She takes a bite of her roll followed by a long gulp of Hawaiian Punch.

Honk honk!

I look at Mom.

"You'd better get going, pumpkin," she says. "Have a great time."

"Tell your daddy Aunt Mona sends him a big kiss," Mona says as I hug her goodbye.

I don't know what to say to Naomi. Her cheeks are flushed and she looks like she might cry.

"Bye, Nao—" I start, but she rushes silently past me and up the stairs to her room.

Dad's van smells like stale Nilla Wafers and socks. Just behind the driver's and passenger's seats is a plaid curtain that blocks my view of the back of the van.

"Are you living in here?" I ask, turning to the curtain.

"Hey! Don't touch that!" he quickly says. "It's a mess back there."

"So, you *are* living in here?" I ask again, handing him his mail. "Is it...okay?"

Flipping through envelopes and advertising flyers, he chuckles to himself. "I guess this has to be my abode for now." He tosses all but two envelopes on the floor in front of me, stuffs one in his jacket pocket, and tosses the other into *my* lap as he looks ahead and pulls off onto the road.

"What's this?" I ask.

"You tell me," he says. "Looks like it's from your swim teacher. Doesn't look like a regular renewal application. What do you think it's about?"

When I hesitate, Dad simply says, "Open her up!"

I take a better look at the envelope, at the word *URGENT* written alongside our address and underlined twice.

Dang, Mrs. Salway!

My heart feels tight in my chest. I know what it's going to say. Or, at least what it's going to *reveal*. That I didn't go to my swim classes last summer. That I cut out the year before just as it was time to do our graduating swim. That I never graduated to Fish. When summer classes start up in a few months, Mom is going to expect me to go, and I haven't told her anything. I haven't even thought about it until now. . . . But then, Dad's much easier about this sort of thing. Maybe if I tell him, he can ease the news to Mom. Maybe she won't get quite as mad.

"Dad?"

"Yeah, kiddo?"

"I need to tell you something."

And I spill it all. Cutting class. My fear of the deep end. The little-kid Polliwogs. Even about Jennifer, Trina, and Melinda.

"Well," he says, putting the van in park. "That's a lot to be holding on to with no one to share it with. Carrying a secret like that could really wear a person out."

I'll say!

He cuts the engine. "You need me to talk to your mom?" he asks.

"You're not mad?" I still don't know what it says in that envelope, but it sounds like Dad's ready to handle whatever it is.

"Look, I'll talk to your mom about this on one condition," he says, and I nod vigorously to let him know that I'll agree to any condition if he's willing to run interference on this one. "No more secrets! Hear me."

And I nod again, only not with the same enthusiasm. After all, I can't come clean about *everything*. Not about Jimmy. But Dad's clearly satisfied that I'm going to keep my part of the deal.

"Let's go," he says, opening his door.

The place isn't as snazzy as the restaurants he usually takes my mom to, but as soon as we walk in I think I may have died and gone to heaven. My head is swirling with the tangy smell of spaghetti sauce, and there's cheesy garlic bread on every table we pass on the way to our own. It takes all my power not to snatch a piece when no one's looking.

Once we're seated, Dad takes a quick look around the room before he turns to me and asks, "You doing all right there, kiddo? This okay?"

He looks thinner than the last time I saw him, but maybe it's just his hair. It's a little longer than he usually keeps it. But no, he does look a little tired. I can't imagine he's getting a peaceful sleep out on the street crammed in the back of the van with cars whizzing by. And I'm sure he must really miss Mom. Judging from his face tonight, I think he's missed me, too.

"It smells so yummy!" I say. "Did you see her spaghetti?" I ask, pointing to the last table we passed. "I'm getting that!"

"Whatever you like. Let's get you a Shirley Temple for starters!" Dad flags down our waiter and I get a wave of sadness, missing dinner out with my parents. I think it's what Mrs. Quakely calls nostalgia. I have what almost feels like an ache in my body as I realize we're probably not going to have any more of those nights together.

Dad quickly turns to the subject of school. About my studies and if I've made any friends yet. Once we've exhausted that subject, I ask him some more questions about the van and what living in there is like.

It takes us clear until dessert before we talk about the real stuff.

"Do you think you and Mom will get back together?" His eyes dart up from his blueberry cheesecake and meet mine. For a moment he says nothing and seems to be seriously considering the question. He raises his eyebrows and smirks.

"Well, kiddo," he says, and sets his fork down. "I guess that's the question of the year, isn't it? Actually, it's something you should probably ask your mom. I think that's going to be up to her. Not me." He takes a bite of cheesecake and stares at the plate as he chews. When he finishes, still looking at the plate, he says, "I didn't leave."

I feel a sting of guilt. Like *I'm* the one who left. After all, I was there in the car with Mom in the middle of the night. I took off *with* her without so much as a "Goodbye, Dad." And for the first time, I realize that he's a little mad at Mom.

"But maybe if you would've let her go to college, maybe she wouldn't have left, maybe..."

"Your mom is a smart lady. She'll do what she thinks is best." He puts his fork down, sits back in the booth, and looks around the restaurant as he speaks. "Look, Stevie, I know that whole bit with the tape recorder...well, that wasn't right. I'll even admit that I'm a bit ashamed of myself for behaving that way. I just thought that maybe your mom was...well, it doesn't matter. It was wrong. And I want to apologize. To you. I've already apologized to your mom, for what it's worth. I guess I still need to talk to your cousin."

He takes a sip of his drink and looks around the room. Seems to be studying the faces of the families, the couples, the gray-haired man seated alone, eating his pizza with a knife and fork. His eyes finally float back to me and he almost looks surprised to find me there.

"Sometimes people can start off wanting the same things, and then...sometimes those things can change." He sighs and tries to force a smile, but it only looks like sadness. It's hard for me to see him this way instead of joking and making fun. I shift in my seat and soon I'm looking around the restaurant myself. At the tables of happy people. There's a family; a mom and dad with a boy my age and a little girl. The girl is holding up a super-long noodle and they all laugh as she stretches her arm higher and higher.

Dad throws the last gulp of his drink down and motions for the waiter to bring him another, then he leans forward to face me, like he's got a secret to tell. I lean in close the same way.

"But you listen to me, kiddo," he says in a half whisper. "Your mom loves you so much and so do I. And nothing is going to change as far as that's concerned, you hear me? We're going to see each other as much as you like and we're going to do all sorts of fun things."

I nod and my smile feels real.

"Hey, what do you say we make a plan to go to Disneyland?" he asks.

"Okay," I say. And I have to laugh to myself. I guess your parents' splitting up is how you get to Disneyland!

"Okay!" He seems to feel better as he digs into the

cheesecake again. "This is so good. You'd better jump in here before I finish it."

I take a bite, and as the sweet berries help make everything a little better, I feel eyes on me. I turn and see the little girl with the spaghetti noodle looking at Dad and me and smiling.

Chapter Twenty-Five

It's an early Saturday morning when I lace up my new skates and hit the park. The basketball courts are empty this time of day. I have the smooth blacktop all to myself. There's hardly a soul in the entire park. No kids in the sand or even on the slide. The swings are still. The orange morning light catches each dewy blade of grass and they sparkle.

I glide onto the empty court and imagine myself in an Olympic arena. I throw my arms out to the sides and crouch low as I pick up more and more speed. I take the corners like a Roller Derby queen defending her lead. I practice jumping, figure eights, skating backward, and spelling out the letter *S* again and again.

Before long, moms with strollers and little kids start to

stream in. They're piling onto the rocket slide, swinging on the monkey bars. Eating sand. Ech. The sun is creeping up high and hot and I'm about to go find a tree and its shade when I hear, "You're good!"

Just outside the entrance of the park, through the chain-link fence, is Ally. She heads for the entrance... on skates! Camel-colored suede skates with purple wheels, an orange brake, and rainbow laces!

She rolls onto the court, past and around me fast. She's doing backward S's, jumping, spinning, and crouching down low on one skate with the other leg extended out front.

She's amazing!

"How do you do that?"

She laughs, straightens, and does a jump and spin, coming down on both feet, arms out to the side. Once she's reached the far end of the court, she turns and skates fast in the other direction before jumping again, spinning, but this time her legs don't come down together and she quickly loses her balance and wipes out.

"Ally!"

A couple of the moms gasp and look on, concerned.

I quickly skate over to her, but by the time I get to her she's already trying to stand. Man, she's a tough one.

"You okay?" I offer her my hand, engaging my brake

so we both don't tumble. She nods, so I pull her up and we roll off the court to the grass. We find a patch to sit on while Ally cleans her scrape with her spit.

"It's not that bad," she says. "I think it's my butt that hurts the most. Ow!" She rubs her bruised backside and we both crack up. "Hey, you're gonna go to John Adams, right?"

"Yeah," I say. It's the first time anyone has asked me where I'm going to junior high in the fall. "You?"

"Uh-huh," she says, smiling. "I hope we get some classes together. I'm kind of nervous about junior high. I hope I don't get lost. It's so much bigger than Walt Whitman."

"It's the ninth graders I hear we have to look out for!"

"Yeah," she says, but quickly changes her tone. "But if anyone tried to dump me in a trash can, they'd be so sorry."

I can't help but giggle at her tough girl rising up.

"I'm serious!" she says. "No way. I don't care what grade they're in!" She can't help but laugh a little, too, hearing herself.

We both spot a little girl sitting alone atop the monkey bars, watching the action from up high.

"Hey! She stole your seat!" Ally says. She laughs and gives me a playful shove. Then, "Tetherball this week?"

I nod. "It's our *last* week."

"Yeah, so you'd better!"

"I will. I promise."

"Shake on it?" She holds her hand out and we shake. Then Ally dusts herself off and stands.

"I better go," she says. "I was supposed to just be cutting through the park on the way to my mom's."

I stand to say goodbye, and I have an idea. Or maybe it's another wish. Whatever it is, I have to gather my courage and put myself out there.

"You know, I'm starting a clubhouse, and I was thinking maybe..." But Ally's brow is knit in a question and I'm pretty sure she thinks I'm dumb. Is a clubhouse a little-kid thing? Shoot. What's wrong with me? I shouldn't have said anything. I'm about to tell her to forget it when her face suddenly brightens.

"Roller Derby Queens!" she says. "The name of our club! What do you think?"

Yeah!

"Yeah!" I say aloud. "I like it!"

And I guess it's 'cause I told Ally about the clubhouse and she was so cool with it that, before I can even consider telling her, or not telling her, a waterfall of sharing comes pouring out of me.

"My parents are separated now, too," I blurt.

Ally's mouth drops open and her eyes go wide as the sea and I think maybe she's going to say something, maybe tell me that it's going to be okay, or maybe that it's *not* going to be okay. I don't know what she's about to say, because once I start talking, I can't stop. I don't give her a chance to offer anything. It's like I have no control over myself, and a flood of feeling and confession and fear and guilt, all kinds of stuff I didn't know was in me, comes rushing out and onto my shoes and the grass and the whole park and...all of Santa Monica. I tell her about how much I didn't want this to happen. How I tried to keep it from happening. How I don't know where my dad is going to live or if he's sad or scared. How I can't imagine what it'll be like without him around.

"I wanna talk to my mom about it, but I don't want to make her feel bad or like she has to worry about *me*. I think she was really unhappy, but I just don't know what to do."

It isn't until Ally reaches out and wipes a tear from my cheek that I realize I'm crying.

"They might get divorced, but you'll be okay. I mean, you said you'll still get to see your dad all the time....I don't know, my dad and me, we have so much more fun now. I don't know about your parents, but mine were fighting like alley cats 24/7. It was awful." She does her best catfight impression, then lets out a snorty laugh. I manage a small chuckle. "You know it has nothing to do with you, right?" I blink the tears back. Blink Ally back into view.

"My dad told me it's *their* relationship that needed a change. Not ours. Nothing about *your* relationship with either of them will change."

I nod. I know she's right about that. I wish I could think of something to say to make her stay. But I know she has to go.

"Listen, if you ever need help navigating life with separated parents," she says with a laugh as she begins to roll away, "I'm the expert!"

As the park fills up, I take to the sidewalks of my neighborhood, snagging handfuls of white wedding flowers from the curbs and navigating the cracked and bumpy sidewalks.

I'm about to turn around and head home when something catches my eye.

A white van. Parked along the side street looking like a big, abandoned refrigerator. There's no doubt about it, it's my dad's.

Sometimes I see his van in the parking lot of Norm's Coffee Shop. And once I skated around to the side of the building and peeked in the window. It wasn't hard to find him. Wide booth in the back corner of the restaurant, table littered in newspapers.

There he can sit back in his vinyl leather throne, read his paper, drink his coffee, be king of the coffee shop.

Staring at the van, it's still hard to imagine that he

actually *lives* in there. How does he move around? Maybe he's in there now reading the paper and having a cup of coffee. I wait and watch. Watch for any small movement, half hoping the side doors of the tin can will fling open and he'll step out into the sunlight in his navy slacks and crisp white shirt. His hair will be slicked back neat and tight above his ears.

I wait.

And wait.

Finally I push off on my skates, head down the sidewalk and across the street. When I get to the van, it feels so still. I put my ear to the side of it but don't hear a thing. There's no way he's in here. If he was, he'd have to be sleeping, and I've never known my dad to sleep in the middle of the day.

I rap on its side, softly at first, and then, when there's still no sound or movement at all, I knock harder. I peer in through the passenger window but can't see past the plaid curtain.

"You need some help, young lady?" I turn fast, almost losing my balance. An elderly man has rolled up behind me on his walker. His curved spine makes his back look big and round, like he's hiding a giant shell under his jacket. He pauses and turns his little turtle head to face me.

"No," I say. "I'm fine. Thanks." I quickly consider

saying *my dad lives here*, but as soon as I think it, I realize how nuts it sounds, so I settle on "No, no help. Thanks." The man lingers a moment. I think he's trying to figure out if I'm up to no good, so I smile brightly and try to look as harmless as possible until he must finally figure I'm no threat and rolls on.

Once the old man is gone, I scan the streets for my dad. Maybe he's gone for a walk or something. I look up and down trying to see any traces of him on foot. Walking back from Surf Liquor with snacks or coming back from the laundromat with his clean wash.

Across from the park I see a row of long-stemmed lilies bursting up between the sidewalk and the curb. The orange of their petals is so vivid you'd swear the color could come off on your fingers. They might be the most beautiful things I've ever seen.

I skate over, reach down, and yank up one lily, then another, then another. I skate down a bit farther and come upon a street flush with pink, yellow, and purple flowers. I snatch up one of every color. I find more white wedding flowers, roses, dandelions. I gather flowers of every color and every length, then skate back to the van. I lift a single lily from my bouquet and slide it between the two side doors. I tuck pansies under the windshield. The side-view mirrors get roses. Wedding flowers frame the tires.

I fill every hinge, every crack, every space I find, with a beautiful flower.

When my hands are finally empty, I turn for home, but when I'm about halfway up the block, I have to turn and look.

The van itself has become a beautiful bouquet. Some-place he can call home.

Chapter Twenty-Six

It's only 10:15 and Mrs. Quakely has already started the waterworks. For the last couple of weeks, she's been going on and on about how there's never been a class like ours and about how much she's going to miss us when we all head off to junior high, but I didn't expect she'd start crying before lunch.

"Oh, Mercedes!" I hear her bellow, and look up to see her swinging Mercedes from side to side (at least I think she's in there somewhere). Her eyes have been leaking all morning. She swaddled me in a bear hug when I came in this morning and gave her the cookies my mom made for her. She didn't totally break down then, but for a moment I thought she might.

"Stevaroni!" she crooned, burying her face in my hair and squeezing me flat. "You'd better visit me!"

"You bet I will."

I can't believe it. *The last day of school!*

The entire week, Mrs. Quakely allowed us free time every day! Free time all day to do whatever we want!

"You made it through the year and you deserve it!" she said.

We can read or draw, play board games or cards, as long as we do it quietly. I've been doing a lot of reading but let Ally rope me into a couple of games of Clue. (Why she *insists* on being Professor Plum I'll never know!)

"Everyone gather around the piano!" Mrs. Quakely calls, dabbing her eyes and studying the clock. "Quick! Let's get one in before recess!"

Ally finds me on the rug and plops down next to me. Rachel and Kim cop a squat on the other side of her.

"Okay? We all settled? C'mon now, there you go. All right!" She taps a few keys before launching into one of our favorite songs. It's trademark super-silly Mrs. Quakely, but even so, we don't lose ourselves in fits of uncontrollable laughter like we did at the beginning of the year. Instead, we push through even the funniest parts, holding it together, and I can hear everyone, including myself, singing louder and fuller than ever before. We're going to miss

Mrs. Quakely and her crazy songs. I know *I* will. I'm going to miss everything about her. I'm definitely coming back to visit.

I'm completely caught up in the song like the rest of the class when I feel what I think is a bug in my hair. I swat at it and soon after I feel something hit my cheek. Too big to be a bug, I wipe the spot where it hit me and it's wet. I turn around and Kenny and Donald are doing their best to contain their laughter. Donald's trying, unsuccessfully, to hide his hand under his thigh, but I can see the plastic straw there.

Spitballs.

I shake my hair and swat at it some more. A tiny, wet wad of paper falls free.

Ugh.

I aim my best death stare at Kenny and Donald, but that only sets them off howling. They can no longer contain themselves.

Without missing a key on the piano, Mrs. Quakely lasers them: "Hey! Behave!" With that, they pull themselves together, but when she turns, they make ugly faces at me while singing the song.

Ally catches that something's going on and swivels around to see what I was looking at. When she spots the class bullies, she scrunches up her face and sticks her tongue out. She didn't see the spitballs, but she knows them well enough to suspect they were up to something.

"Were those jerks bothering you again?" she asks as we file out for recess.

"They don't have anything better to do," I say. Then I point to the tetherball pole. "Game?" Ally's face lights up and she tears off for the pole. I'm fast on her heels.

We've only had a chance to play one game before Kenny, Donald, and their favorite chew toy, Marcus, saunter over.

"So, Marcus's going to Paul Revere, not John Adams. I think you guys need to make it official or else his heart's gonna be broken." Kenny pushes Marcus forward and he stumbles a bit in an effort to avoid falling on me.

"Well, Kenny, actually I'm fine. I'm fine." Marcus forces a laugh as he pulls the heel of his shoe back on where it's come loose.

Donald barks, "Kiss her, Marcus. Do it!" He shoves Marcus, and this time his feet aren't quick enough and he trips and falls into me. Caught off guard, I lose my balance as Marcus knocks me down and falls *on top of me*.

"Oh, shoot! I'm sorry." Marcus is apologizing like crazy as he tries to stand, but his knee is in my lap and I'm tumbling backward.

We're twisted in a ball of limbs, struggling to untangle

ourselves as Kenny and Donald look on pointing and laughing loudly. Doing their best to draw a crowd. When I've finally freed myself from Marcus and am on my knees trying to stand, I see that they've gotten their wish. Half the playground has gathered.

"Hey, Stevie, I'm really sorry," Marcus keeps saying. There's a tear, surrounded by a deep grass stain, over his left knee. His polyester button-up shirt has come untucked from his pants. As I dust myself off, bits of dried grass fall from my hair like snow.

"Dang. Your hair is like a dust mop!" Kenny says, cackling. I don't give it any thought. My legs are moving before my brain has even had a chance to make heads or tails of everything around me. I march over to Kenny and with my face an inch from his, I start in.

"You know, the only good thing about going to the same junior high as you next year is getting to see the ninth graders kick your sorry butt. Bullies like you are always the first ones to get it."

"Yeah! You wish!" Kenny sneers.

"You'd better believe I do." I turn my back on him and, little do I know at the time, but jerk head Kenny lifts one of his dirty Keds and is about to literally kick me in the butt, when Marcus grabs ahold of his raised foot. Hearing the commotion of the crowd, I turn around just in time to see Marcus lift Kenny's leg and throw him backward onto the grass. He goes down hard! The crowd loves it. Kenny is on his back, clutching his left arm with his right.

"My arm!" he shouts, writhing around on the ground.

Some kids laugh. Some gasp. Mercedes goes running for the front office. Donald reaches down to offer Kenny a hand, but he screams at him.

"Get away from me, you idiot!"

Marcus, in what just might be a state of shock, stands over Kenny, almost daring him to get up and try something like that again.

"I swear I'm gonna kick your ass, Marcus!" the squirming worm cries from the grass.

Marcus nods at him, and I can't tell if he's saying yeah, you probably will, or dream on, brother. He turns to me, plucks a twig from my hair. And we head back to the classroom.

"Maybe he will kick my butt," he says, shrugging and chewing on his lip. "But I don't even think I care. That was so worth it."

The remainder of the last day is spent with everyone's running around getting signatures from friends in their yearbooks. Needless to say, I'm not doing any running anywhere. I don't have a lot of signatures to collect. But I do get Ally to sign my book, and I'm really surprised when a few people actually ask me to sign theirs. Marcus is one of them.

"I want to write something in yours, too," he says.

"We'll meet again!"

And he draws a picture of a Herculean version of himself with bulging biceps!

When it's finally time to go, Mrs. Quakely folds me into her arms and whispers in my ear.

"I'm proud of you, Stevie. Coming here new wasn't easy. Keep letting folks see you. Keep sharing your fun," she says. She pulls back, looks me in the eye. "You got me?"

"I got you."

From behind me, Ally, joined by Rachel and Kim, throw their arms around Mrs. Quakely (and me) and Ally yells, "Group hug!" as we all get in one last squeeze.

It was Naomi's last day of school, too, so she and some friends are having a celebratory slumber party at Sandra's. Mom and I pop up some popcorn and settle into the Friday Night Movie, just the two of us!

"We're *both* out of school for the summer," Mom says. "I promise to do my best with scheduling when I sign up for classes next year, but at least for now, we can get back to our Friday Night Movies!"

"Yay!"

We both cheer, grab fistfuls of popcorn, and lie back, enjoying the film.

The next morning, Mom shakes me awake.

"Throw some clothes on. I'm taking the ladies to brunch to celebrate the official first day of summer vacation! You, me, Naomi, and Mona."

I sit up, wipe the sleep from my eyes, and as I'm pulling my shorts on, hear Mom on the phone, laughing with Mona. But by the time I get to the kitchen, dressed but still groggy, she's no longer talking to Mona and she's no longer laughing.

"And she didn't say where she was going?" She rubs her temple with her thumb. "Jimmy? Who is Jimmy?"

Chapter Twenty-Seven

Sandra said Naomi left early this morning with some-one named Jimmy. Do *you* know anyone named Jimmy? I've never heard her mention that name. Stevie, do you think Naomi was angry? That she'd...? I know we argued recently, but it wasn't *that* bad." Mom leans forward on the steering wheel as she drives, like having her face closer to the windshield will help her spot Naomi. She's chewing on her bottom lip and looks so worried. "Six in the morning! He got her at six! She said she doesn't know where they were going, but... I couldn't tell if that was true or..."

My heart sinks into my stomach and I feel cold and light-headed.

Did Naomi actually run away with Jimmy? Is she gone?

No, it's not possible. She wouldn't leave *me*. Would she?

I don't know what to say to Mom. Do I tell her I know Jimmy? That I was there when they first met? Maybe if I'd told Mom about Jimmy at the start, Naomi wouldn't have run away with him. That is, if she even has. Please, please, please don't let that be true.

I look over the sidewalks as we drive through Santa Monica and then Venice. I search the streets for the Chevy Camaro.

I guess I *could* tell Mom about Jimmy's car. Man, I don't wanna be a snitch!

"Damnit!" Mom says, and bangs on the steering wheel. "Okay, we're heading back home. I need to call her mom."

When we get home, I run to the door first and let us in with my key. Mom goes straight to the kitchen, but I don't hear her call Auntie Flo right away. I hear her pull out a chair and just sit in silence. I know she doesn't want to make that call. To tell her sister that, under her watch, Naomi may have run away again.

Elvis appears, pushing up against my ankles, begging for me to hold him, so I reach down and take him in my arms. As I do, my key swings forward and I tuck it into my top so it doesn't hit him. And then I remember...the key around my neck reminds me...

Holding the cat close to my chest, I run upstairs to Naomi's room. Elvis squirms and jumps free and runs down the hall. Naomi's gold key still dangles on the gold chain hanging from the nail in the wall. I did *not* want to violate her trust this way, but if she's run away, her diary will tell us where she is, and we can bring her back home safely. I go to the foot of her bed and reach through folders and socks but can't feel the hardcover binding. I push through more clothes and paperbacks, magazines, pens. It isn't there.

Think, Stevie.

I look over every surface, in every corner. Where could it be?

You have spy blood.

I lie down on Naomi's bed and take a deep breath. Let it go. I try to *be* Naomi. I'm in bed. I'm about to go to sleep. I just wrote my last entry, clicked my diary closed and locked. Where do I hide it?

Without thinking, I roll over onto my stomach and reach my hand between the mattress and box spring and my finger brushes something. A book. I pull it free. Soft blue background. Shining gold peacock. Matching gold lock. Her diary.

I sit up and am about to put the key in the lock but stop and look at where the key had been hanging. To the photo on the wall that the nail is holding up. It's the one of the light-skinned lady with the afro. But it's not just a photo, it's a flyer.

Black Panther Party's
Community Service Festival
and Food Giveaway

It goes on to talk about music and guest speakers. The star of the event must be the lady in the photo: *Angela Davis*. This is what Naomi had asked Mom about. She'd really wanted to go, but Mom said no way. I look at the date. And, sure enough, it's today.

A banner announcing the festival stretches high and wide above a large field where women and men and boys and girls of every age mingle. Musicians play on the stage while some dance, and others just watch and listen, heads bobbing. White tents on either side of the field sell crafts and offer food. Children sit cross-legged in small circles on the grass eating corn.

"There's a spot!"

I point to a tiny space along the curb between a yellow VW van and a green pickup truck. While Mom struggles to squeeze the Pinto in, I scan the sea of people for Naomi. I don't know. I think this is going to be impossible. Finding

Naomi is going to be like finding a needle in a stack of needles.

"How do we know where to find her?"

But Mom looks determined. She pulls the parking brake and slings her purse over her shoulder. "Let's go," she says.

Three men in African-styled clothing pound drums with their bare hands. The music is intense: whip fast and then suddenly slowed down to skipping beats, dragging thumps, like sleepy feet moving up stairs. One of the men calls out but I can't understand what he says. The other men repeat the call, and the drumming intensifies, picks up pace again. Throughout, their faces are calm as they look only at one another, speaking some silent language, chins pulsing forward in a gentle rhythm.

As soon as we hit the grass I get a whiff of spicy chicken, of mac and cheese, and of something buttery and sweet.

"Can we get something to eat?" I ask, but Mom has no time for me or my appetite. She lasers in on the white tent tops off to the side, grabs hold of my hand, and moves swiftly through the crowd.

"Don't lose me," she says.

A wall of people pressing forward block my view of the food booths entirely but don't keep the aromas from circling my head. I think I'm salivating.

Mom pulls me through a narrow space in the line and zips to the front. Behind the tables, food servers ladle beans and greens into paper bowls, scurrying about at rapid speed. Mostly all of them are women, but peppered in are some teenage boys and girls.

"Excuse me?" Mom tries to get the attention of a young freckled woman with a crown of tight orange curls. She's loading three paper bowls with food and doesn't even look up when Mom speaks.

"Excuse me?" Mom says again, this time louder and with an authority I've only heard her use when even I know I've been out of line. The woman looks up but still doesn't speak or stop moving.

"Do you know a young girl named Naomi Andrews? Fifteen? Is she here?"

The woman shrugs. Mom shakes her head in frustration and pulls me through a break in the tables and behind the food stations. In the commotion of people loading food, emptying cans, and hauling ice, Mom stops another woman and is trying to describe Naomi to her when coming our way, carrying a large silver tray in oven-mitted hands, I spot my cousin.

"Mom." I shake her arm, pointing, and she stops mid-sentence when she sees Naomi. Her hand, which has been gripping my wrist for the last twenty minutes, finally releases and she moves so fast toward her that I brace myself for a slap and a scream and the something awful that I just know is about to occur. Naomi stops in her tracks when she sees Mom. I'm slow to walk over to them, afraid for what might happen. They stand there a beat before Naomi finally speaks.

"I'm sorry, Aunt Kitty." I've never seen Naomi look so little.

"Yeah?" Mom cocks her head to the side. "Looks more like you're doing what you want to do to me." Even from where I stand, I can see that Mom's nose is flared as she stares at Naomi.

"I—I know you told me not to, but I...but it wasn't what you thought, and I knew—I knew that if you—you understood—" Naomi stammers.

"You lied, Naomi. You went against my word."

"And I'm sorry for that. I really am—"

Mom's shaking her head now. A face and a stance I know well. She's disappointed.

"How can I ever trust you?"

"But—but you thought that the Panthers were bad. And they're not," she pleads. "Look around. Please."

Mom's still slicing Naomi to bits with her laser eyes, but I do take a look around, at the stage, the performers onstage, the food tables. I can't see what's so bad.

"They're not what you think. If they were, it'd be one thing, but—"

"The point is you went behind my back. And that you *lied*. Your mother would be livid. She trusted me to care for you after what happened in Boston."

"I was suffocating in Boston. My mom couldn't understand. I was just trying to *do* something. I couldn't sit back and just *watch* anymore." Naomi is shaking now as the tears fall fast over her face. "I shouldn't have lied, but… but…you weren't going to let me come, Aunt Kitty. And doing this work for the community, it's important. It's the first time I've felt like I have something to offer. Like I'm making a difference." Mom doesn't interrupt, and her face has softened. I see her eyes move past Naomi and into the crowd, taking them in. "I'm not saying it's right to lie, but…I know you understand."

I didn't see him approach, but suddenly, Jimmy is stepping up to Mom with his hand outstretched.

"Mrs. Morrison? I'm Jimmy Cole." Mom shifts her attention from Naomi for a moment and takes a deep breath but quickly turns her eyes back to Naomi while Jimmy speaks. "I understand that you're angry. You have every reason to be angry, but it isn't really Naomi you should be mad at, it's me. I told her how important it was for her to be here—"

"She made her own decision," Mom says. She shakes her head at the ground before looking up at Jimmy. "And I don't know you. This is between my niece and me."

"Yes, yes, you're right about that. But please know that the work that Naomi has done—putting in after-school hours and her weekends—it's meant so much to this chapter and to the community. She may have gone against your word, but...but you have to know that it wasn't for nothing."

Mom doesn't say anything. She sighs heavily and her eyes seem to have drifted to a group of little kids playing duck, duck, goose.

"Please, Aunt Kitty. Look around. See for yourself," Naomi says. When Mom looks back at her, Naomi takes a deep breath. "I know it's a lot to ask, and you can say no, of course, but please, *please* can I just finish up my shift? Then I'll leave. I'll accept whatever punishment. I deserve it. I lied. I know. It's just...we're already short on people and there's no one else coming in to help until two."

Another teenage girl runs by carrying two jugs of bright colored liquid.

"Whatchoo doing, Naomi? C'mon, girl!" she says as she runs past us to the food tables.

Naomi looks at my mom, and Mom takes a deep breath and lets it out with a shake of her head.

"Give me that," she says, nodding at the tray Naomi's holding. "Is it hot?" The two of them slip the potholders and tray into Mom's hands.

"Thank you, Auntie," Naomi says, beaming, and runs for the food tents. Mom follows and motions to me.

"Come on, Stevie," she says. "Looks like we have some work to do."

Behind the counter, Naomi is pouring ice into cups and taking food orders from the crowd. She turns to me as I enter.

"Can you grab that empty tin?" Her chin points to an aluminum tray scraped clean except for a few remnants of caramelized sweet potatoes along the edges.

"Quick. This is hot," Mom says.

I pull the tray free, making room for Mom to put the new tray in its place. She lifts the aluminum top and puts it on top of the tin I'm holding.

"You can put that right around the back," Naomi says, indicating a stack of emptied food tins just behind the food tent. Mom grabs a couple of paper bowls and starts helping Naomi serve food and pour drinks.

Mountains of tins are stacked behind the tents. I carefully balance mine on top, then go back to help Mom and Naomi. I empty trash and stack cans of soda. Naomi shows me how to make a pitcher of punch. After a while Mom's laughing with strangers and she looks so happy. I can't remember the last time I saw her enjoying herself with friends. With her sisters, maybe, and then with Clarence. But watching her now, I realize it's Mom who's needed some new friends.

I'm taking another empty tin to the back when I see a girl walk up and add two more to the pile. She has one long cornrow spiral that travels in circles, getting smaller and smaller until it ends in one long braid coming out of the top of her head.

"Hi," she says, sticking her face behind our tent, studying the trays of food, the cooler of cold drinks. "Ooh, you got hush puppies!" I look for what she's talking about and see a tray full of what look like giant brown crumb balls.

I shrug and drop my tin on top of the others. "What're hush puppies?"

"You ain't never had a hush puppy?" She looks at me like I am definitely from Mars, then goes to Naomi and tugs at her sleeve.

"What is it, Kendra?" Wait, Naomi knows her? How?

"She ain't never had a hush puppy," the girl says, pointing in my direction. "You think maybe—?"

Naomi turns to me with a look of astonishment. "Seriously, Stevie?" I shrug and shake my head. I still don't know what the big deal is. In a flash, she's loaded some napkins with four of the big crumb balls and poured us two cups of grape punch. "Here you go. You two take a break and eat." She points to the grass behind the tent. I follow Kendra and we both sit.

"I can't believe you never had a hush puppy. These are my *favorite*!" She hands me two balls and one of the napkins and we both bite into the sweet cornmeal. It's like cake and cornbread all rolled into one crispy shell. At the same time we both let out an "mmmm!" That sets us both laughing.

"Good, right?" She nods at me.

"Mm-hmm!" I say, and shove the rest of it into my mouth. When I finish chewing, I say, "Your hair is so cool."

Her hand travels to her head and she smiles as she traces the long, flat braid and then tugs on the end of the one that comes out the top.

"Thanks! I like *yours*!" she says. "It's so pretty."

I reach up and touch my cloud of curls. "Really? Thanks."

Our eyes drift away from the commotion of people on the field, from the swarm of folks asking Mom and Naomi for something salty to eat or cool to drink. We turn and stare out at the stretch of untouched green grass behind the tents as we drink and eat. For a long time we don't say anything at all. And the silence is nice.

"Ooh! Look!" Kendra reaches for the grass and snatches

up a big, fluffy dandelion puff. "Here," she says, shoving it in my hand, and then yanking another puffy flower from the grass for herself. We both give each other a real serious look before closing our eyes and making our silent wishes.

I make the same wish I always make. *I wish I had a friend.* Then I think about Ally...and realize maybe I do. Maybe it's time to wish for something new.

When we open our eyes, we blow the puffs with all our might. I have to keep blowing at a few stubborn pieces of fluff.

"Almost!" Kendra says. "Blow harder!" I give it everything I've got, and the last little pieces float away. I hold my bald stem up to Kendra.

"Wishes on the way!" she declares, and tosses her stem deep into the green.

The music stops and someone speaks into the microphone. It's so loud I grab my ears, but it's too muffled for me to completely understand what they're saying. Something about everybody gathering to the front. That the speakers are about to begin. People quickly turn from the tents and tables and move toward the stage.

"C'mon, Stevie!" Naomi says, and motions me to her. "We gotta go listen." Mom is talking to a woman wearing a camouflage jacket and glasses who has come into our tent and seems to be taking over.

"I got it. You go on," she says, smiling. Mom thanks her and turns to me.

I jump to my feet and before I can say anything to Kendra, she's up and throwing her arms around me. She gives me a quick hug and then runs back in the direction she came, her long braid swinging from side to side.

As I wave goodbye to the woman behind the food table and cross to the field, she says, "You were a big help today, little sis! Thank you."

We squeeze our way through the thick of people, shoulder to shoulder with the crowd. Just when I'm about to whine about my sore feet and the blazing sun, Naomi grabs hold of Mom's hand and leads her even deeper into the mass of bodies, toward the front. I hold on tight to Mom's hand and squeeze through behind them.

A petite lady no taller than me screeches into the microphone for a good twenty minutes. She's saying that we have rights but that we're not being treated fairly. That we have to fight for justice. I can't make out all of it, but folks shout their approval whenever she pauses and cheer when she finally finishes. I think she said something important.

A reverend takes the podium and asks us to bow our heads. I tilt my head down, closing my eyes, but can't help but lift my head a little and crack an eye open just to be sure I'm not the only one doing it. Mom's head is bowed.

Naomi doesn't bow her head. She defiantly faces the stage with eyes shut. The crowd is silent, their faces tranquil. Some of their mouths move silently as the reverend speaks of love. About its power. I drop my head and close my eyes.

"Amen," we all say.

When I lift my head and open my eyes, the woman from Naomi's flyer is there standing next to him. Naomi screams. The entire crowd erupts. Screams, shouts, applause.

Angela.

I think she's blushing from the outpouring of love directed at her. When she looks up and smiles, even from where we stand, I can see she has a gap in her teeth like Mom's friend Clarence. She is the queen of the afros today. And I'm proud that my mom doesn't wear a wig anymore. That her hair is full and natural. And for the first time, I'm proud of my big hair, too.

She speaks for almost an hour, the crowd hanging on every word she says. I can't see her too well. Tall bodies that keep shifting their feet are constantly blocking me. And while I can't really understand all that she's talking about, the rest of the crowd does. They're all nodding and shouting, and I can feel the audience, as if they were one, leaning in to hear her better. Sometimes everyone gets so excited, clapping and yelling, that she can't get a word in at all. Even Naomi calls out to her, saying, "Yes!" and "Right on!"

Mom, like the rest of the audience, is leaning forward, trying not to let a single word pass her by.

Naomi turns to me, speaking loudly so I can hear her above the crowd.

"Can you see?"

I shake my head and Naomi grabs hold of my hand, pulls me in front of her, and with her hands on either side of my waist, lifts me up. It's only maybe a foot off the ground, but I can see Angela better now. Her voice is clear and full of passion.

"I am no longer accepting the things I cannot change. I am changing the things I cannot accept!"

Applause rolls through the crowd.

But Naomi's arms can't hold me up.

"Girl, you're heavier than you look!" she says, and laughs. And then, suddenly, I feel someone else's hands on my waist, lifting me up high. It's Jimmy.

"Let's get you up there, little cuz," he says, lifting me up and onto his shoulders. Now I can see over the whole crowd.

As I try to get comfortable on Jimmy's shoulders, something jabs me in my pocket. When I reach inside I find the orange button with the big black panther on the front that the man at the mall gave me.

ALL POWER
TO THE
PEOPLE

I pin it to the front of my T-shirt, then turn and look behind me. People every shade of brown, and some white, are stretched out across the lawn of the park facing the stage, chins high, faces bright and beaming. I've never seen so many afros in all my life. Women, men, and even kids my age and younger have their naturals combed out full and round. A beautiful field of dandelions.

Chapter Twenty-Eight

Mom and I joined Naomi in working two more Black Panther events over the summer. Kendra and I were put in charge of beverages. We made all the pitchers of punch for all the stands, and we walked through the crowd offering cups of ice water.

I still don't think Mom's had the nerve to tell Aunt Flo about any of it, or how she's allowing Naomi to participate in the events. I wonder if she ever will. In the meantime, we're careful to avoid any Panther talk around Mona!

"C'mon, Stevie. Let me give you a ride." Mom's been looking at me with the worried face all morning. It's my first day of junior high and I think *she* thinks I should be nervous. But I'm not. Like the rest of the kids starting the seventh grade today, I've heard all about how the eighth and ninth graders are mean to "scrubs" (that's us). How they'll dump you in the trash can if you cross through their quad. But I'm not sweating any of it. Anything will be better than last year. And besides, over the summer Ally and I studied self-defense moves just in case anybody tries.

"You're *sure* you don't want me to braid your hair?" Mom asks.

Naomi looks up from dusting blue shadow on her eyelids and smiles at me. I can't believe it's been a whole year since she came to live with us. It feels like no time at all, but also like she's been here forever.

"Your hair looks beautiful, cuz," she says.

"I think it looks beautiful, too," Mom says. "I just want you to be your most comfortable today."

"It's the other folks who aren't comfortable," says Naomi.

"You know what I mean," says Mom, rolling her eyes. "But all that teasing. Who wants that?"

"Sticks and stones," Naomi says, smiling at me again.

"Yes, yes. It's up to you, Stevie. Whatever you want. But I can braid it if you like."

I reach up and touch my large, airy natural. It's soft and it's tall.

"No," I say. "I'm good."

I enter the halls and it's so much bigger than elementary

school. There are so many more kids. Still, I don't have any trouble finding my locker, my first-period class, the bathroom.

I pass Kenny and Donald in the hall, trying to open their lockers, faces beet red with embarrassment. They try to pretend they don't see me as they take turns twisting and turning the combination lock and tugging on the door that refuses to open. Ha! It only took me one try.

The bell rings as I'm approaching my first-period class. I'm about to go inside when Jennifer runs up to me. She's got the matching red cheeks of most of the seventh graders today. The dead giveaway that she's beyond nervous.

"Hey, Stevie!" she says. I look behind her, expecting to see Tweedle Dee and Tweedle Dum, but it looks like she's solo.

"Hey," I say, and I don't try to fill the awkward space that follows. I let it lie there and allow her to fill it up. Or not.

"Um...I was going to call you," she says.

Call me? I thought for sure she'd lost my number. But I don't say anything. I just look at her as if to say *And?*

But she doesn't explain that she lost my number or that she forgot she had laryngitis or that her fingers stopped working so she couldn't dial. Instead, she quickly jumps to another subject.

"Is this your first period?" She clutches her books to

her chest and nods at the door that I'm *clearly* about to walk through.

"Uh-huh," I say. "English."

"Oh, I have—" she starts, but before she can finish, Trina and Melinda appear. And, I'm not sure if it's my imagination, but Jennifer seems to visibly shrink before my eyes. Trina doesn't seem to be fazed by the new school or by being one of the "little kids" here, but Melinda's got the red cheeks.

"What's wrong with you, Jennifer? French is down there," she scolds, looking at Jennifer like she is stupid. She shakes her head dismissively and turns to me, eyeing my hair with that "I smell skunk" face, then motioning to her minions with her chin. Before she takes off, she reaches her hand into my afro and moves her fingers about like she's searching for coins in her handbag.

"Bye, fluffy," she says. And without even a moment's thought, I have grabbed hold of her wrist and lifted it from my hair.

I hear Jennifer gasp.

"You mind?" I say.

A couple of girls walking past and into my classroom burst into laughter.

"Ooh, she told you!" one of them says as they continue inside.

Her friend with the afro puffs adds, "That'll teach you to keep your hands to yourself."

Trina's face is redder than Mars. She shakes her arm free and heads off with Melinda on her tail.

Before Jennifer can utter a word, Ally runs up and links my arm.

"Yes! We have the same homeroom!" She doesn't even seem to notice Jennifer. She reaches into her book bag, pulls out a *Tiger Beat* magazine, and shoves it into my hand. "For decorating the clubhouse! I'll save you a seat next to mine." She runs in and I turn back to Jennifer. The flush of her cheeks has traveled down her neck and lit up her collarbone.

"You'd better go. Don't wanna be late on the first day," I say.

"Yeah, right. I—I know," she stutters.

"Jennifer!" Trina barks from down the hall.

"Well, maybe I'll see you at lunch."

I smile and give her a half nod before going in and taking a seat next to my friend.

Chapter Twenty-Nine

Dad said he doesn't want me to get sick of Italian food, so instead of a restaurant, this weekend we're hitting the beach. I couldn't believe he suggested it.

"Have I ever gone to the beach with you?" I ask him, trying to remember if maybe when I was a little kid we played in the sand together or something. But if we did, I had to be *really* little. I cannot imagine my dad in swim trunks!

"Of course!" he says, laughing. "Well, to be fair, it's probably been a while. In fact... when's the last time I was at the beach?"

"I saw those legs last Halloween. It must've been back in the Stone Age, 'cause wooo! Somebody needs a tan!"

"Oh, you're a joker today, huh? Okay, okay."

Dad picks me up at noon and when we hit the parking lot, I can see that it's already pretty crowded. The start of school never stops anyone from hitting the beach on the weekends in Santa Monica as long as the weather is nice—and today, it's 82 degrees and clear blue skies. But it's breezier on the beach than I'd hoped, and the water looks choppy.

"You still want me to give you those boogie board lessons?" I ask.

"Absolutely!"

We drop our bag and towels on a clear patch of sand not too far from the water, and Dad grabs hold of my hand.

"Ready, kiddo?"

I nod and together we run for the waves.

There's no one else in the water and once I'm up to my waist in it, I can see why. The waves are pretty big and rough. As I try to make my way out a little deeper so I can get behind the breaking waves, I get knocked down again and again. Finally I'm out just far enough. I set myself up in the perfect position and a big wave comes up behind just as I'm jumping on the board. It lifts me up and pushes me across the water, all the way to the shore. When I jump up, I see Dad in the ocean, arms raised high over his head, fists pumping the air in triumph. Muffled by the sound of crashing waves, I can still make out, "Way to go, kiddo!"

Dad's an expert bodysurfer. As soon as he sees a wave cresting behind him, he starts swimming for shore, and before you know it, the wave has caught up to him and pulled him with it all the way to shore. No board necessary.

"I still want to see how you use this thing," he says after he's ridden a few waves in and when he's found his way back to me in the ocean.

"Well, it's similar to what you do without a board," I say.

"Yeah, but...tools," he says, holding the board up and looking at it curiously. "I'm not the best with tools. You're going to have to go easy on me," he jokes.

I show him just how to position himself on the board. The first time he tries, he's way too far back on the board, and when the wave comes, the board juts up and bounces away from him. The next time, the wave knocks him off the board and he gets dunked under completely. He bobs back up laughing.

"Okay, now, you didn't tell me I was going to have to look like a fool!"

I crack up. He does look silly, but instead I say, "You don't! Just be patient. You'll get it."

"I think the ocean's making fun of me!" Then he points to the boogie board. It's flown up and behind me.

"I'll get it," I say, and make my way to the board, but

the tossing waves are pushing it farther out and pretty soon the water is way up to the top of my chest. I'm afraid to go much farther. I won't be able to touch the ground.

I turn back to Dad.

"I think it's too far," I say. But he squints back at me, unable to hear, so I repeat, "I don't think I can get it. It's too far!" At that moment, I realize that he isn't looking at me, but past me, and not at the board. He's looking past me and *up*. Then, lunging forward for me. I turn just in time to see a huge wave crest over my head, and before I can think of what to do, it's come crashing down on me.

Now, this isn't the first time I've been knocked down by a big wave, but usually I pop right back up like one of those inflatable clowns you punch in the face. This time, however, isn't like any other. Partially 'cause I didn't see it coming, and mostly because it's just a killer wave. A killer wave on a mean beach day. Rough and ready waves. Ready to make mincemeat out of a poor sucker like me.

SLAM!

The wave knocks me to the ocean's floor, and I feel my thigh scrape against the rough sand. I tumble and tumble round and round like a penny in a washing machine. I'm holding my breath, and without meaning to, I open my eyes—all I see is murky brown and seaweed. I'm being tossed in a nasty sand salad.

When I finally bob back up and my face hits the open air, I suck up all the oxygen I can fit in my lungs. It feels so good, and I'm relieved to be above the surface of the water again. So happy to be able to breathe. To be okay. I look over the water and I don't see the boogie board, so I'm about to turn to face the shore, to look for the board and for Dad, when I realize for the first time that my feet aren't touching the bottom. I stretch my right foot down, certain that the earth must be just below my pointed toes, but it touches nothing. I stretch the other foot, reaching, reaching, all the while doing my best not to let my chin dip below the surface. I still can't feel the bottom. Everything in me tenses up.

I can't touch the bottom. And I can't swim. I'm gonna sink. I'm gonna drown. I flap my arms against the water in an attempt to keep myself afloat. I kick my legs back and forth. I'm not moving forward. I may even be moving farther into the sea. I'm reaching for air. I just know it's going to be taken from me any minute. I twist and do my best to flap my arms so they'll take me to shore. But what am I doing? Stop flapping, Stevie! Swim! Remember your lessons. I lower my arms, try to tread water. My chin is in the water and, even moving as fast as I am, I can feel my whole body trembling. I don't wanna drown!

Through all my frantic splashing, I see Dad a few feet in front of me in the water.

"Stevie," he's saying. "It's okay. Just try to relax."

"I can't feel the bottom!" I shout.

"It's okay," he says, voice calmer than I've ever heard it. "Just come to me. Slowly."

"I can't!" I say. "I don't know how to swim."

"But kiddo...you do," he says, and smiles. "You're swimming now."

I don't know what the heck he's talking about. I don't swim. I'm a Polliwog. I kick my legs like crazy and my hands churn the surface of the water.

"That's it," he says. "Keep doing what you're doing, but slow down a little and part the water with your hands. That's it. Keep kicking. Keep your hands going. You're doing it, kiddo."

Before I know it, I'm right in front of my dad. He stretches his arm out and grabs hold of me. Carries me a few feet toward the shore before he says, "You did it. You swam!" Then he starts to let go of me. I grab him tight, but he peels me off him. "It's okay," he laughs. "It's okay."

I push my legs straight below me and my feet touch the soft, silty earth.

Author's Note

Like Stevie's relationship with her mom, my mom was my everything. As her only child, I got all of her attention, all of the doting, all of the Christmas presents, the bedtime stories, the snuggles. I thought she was the moon and the sun. She had a big Afro and the prettiest smile. She was warm and kind, and everyone was charmed by her. She was also a woman who had been raised to please. To not make waves. To be a good wife and mother. In the world she grew up in, there were rules that most adhered to in terms of a "woman's place." My parents were married when she was still relatively young, and those unspoken "rules," while not uttered, were very much present when they took their vows. But when the women's liberation movement of the 1970s took hold, the foundation of my parents' union would be rocked.

And it would rock the world I had come to know and was only just beginning to understand.

Although this is a deeply personal story to me, Stevie's story is her own and many events were either invented or exaggerated to make a point, and in order to tell her story, some events and timelines were adjusted. These things are minor to me and less important than what was happening to Stevie and the coming of age of an eleven-year-old girl.

Still, many of my own perceptions of the time have informed Stevie.

Glamorous movie stars of the 1940s, of black-and-white movies, mostly white starlets, had defined beauty and elegance for me. They were the epitome of what was attractive, what I should strive to be, and what the world perceived as the perfect woman.

When my teenage cousin, a modern young woman, came to live with us, the revolution, which saw women burning their bras and demanding equal treatment to men, walked directly into our house and took a seat.

My cousin also opened the windows of our life and let in the "Black Is Beautiful" movement. Suddenly, women like Chaka Khan and Tamara Dobson were in my eyeline. Women who were undeniably beautiful. Women who felt fiercely independent. Women who looked more like me.

As I grappled with new understandings of what a woman

was and what she could be, and as my mother began living this change, my dad was still firmly stuck in 1963. He expected his small corner of the world to stay there with him. But we didn't. Nor did the rest of the world.

Change can be difficult, particularly for those who don't see the need for it. And though we might not always be able to make those we love understand our need for change, we can move forward with compassion, doing our best to bring them along with us.

Acknowledgments

When I started this book, centering on women and girls and the changes of the 1970s, I hadn't anticipated digging into my relationship with my dad. But as the character of the father emerged, he seemed so peculiar and off-putting (former CIA agent, a little distant, big-time chauvinist) that even though this was somewhat true to his personality, I felt the need that he and Stevie bond. I had to look deeper into my own relationship with my dad. Finding the moments of when we connected didn't come naturally, but once uncovered, I realized they had always been there. We shared important times together, formative times that helped me become the woman I am today. What an unexpected gift. Thank you, Dad. I love you.

I will forever be thankful to my agent, Marc Gerald. My friend and champion. You believed in me even before

I did, and you gave me the necessary shove when I truly needed it.

To my editors, Naomi Colthurst and Nikki Garcia, I cannot thank you enough for your patience. Through the many life events and *world* events that pushed and pulled at us during the writing of this book, you stayed with me, offering wisdom and much needed guidance.

Alvina Ling, Milena Blue Spruce, Asmaa Alsse, and everyone at Little, Brown Books for Young Readers and Penguin Random House, thank you for your support throughout.

Thank you, Brian Dunn. I can always count on you.

Jim Krusoe, I know we connected late in the game on this one but simply connecting with you again means the world to me.

Lana and Nico, you are my moon and stars.

And, most importantly, to Alex. My sounding board, my wise man, my truth compass. Thank you. I love you.

31901069406355